MEMORY CLINIC

MEMORY CLINIC

Steven Earnshaw

ROMAN *Books*
www.roman-books.co.uk

ISBN 978-93-83868-19-3

Typeset in Adobe Garamond Pro

First published in 2016

1 3 5 7 9 8 6 4 2

British Library Cataloguing in Publication Data.
A catalogue record for this book is available from the British Library.

Publisher: Suman Chakraborty

ROMAN Books
26 York Street, London W1U 6PZ, United Kingdom
Unit 120, Park Plaza, South Block, Ground Floor, 71 Park Street, Kolkata 700016, WB, India
www.roman-books.co.uk | www.romanbooks.co.in

Printed and bound in India by
Replika Press Pvt Ltd

Contents

Acknowledgments

Lackington's Magazine, 'The Whale of Penlan Tork'; *The Wrong Quarterly*, 'Scar'; *Squawk Back*, 'Iconoclasm of Modern Funeral Vignettes'; *Tears in the Fence*, 'Johannes Boanerges'; *Pif*, 'The King of Ivy'; *The Warwick Review*, 'Correspondence'; *Lab Lit*, 'Zeroth'

Scar

When we are fascinated we extrapolate from scraps, fantasise, claw at the surface of the woman desired. If we had been born into a different age, Melissa would wear the scar on her face proudly, like a wedding ring. Here, she is curious to me, and out of all colleagues, she is the attractive one, a purely aesthetic fetish, engaged by Melissa's careless attitude to time and fashion, her demeanour being what it is. I know nothing of her doings where we are, at work, and rarely see her outside, except I know she has a husband and children, the mere appendages of an outward conformity for which she has no time. Inside, and perhaps the manner is hidden from herself, she galumphs charmingly in a thoroughly heterodox style, bearing her *ressentiment* in a cultured way which I presume, mostly in the right, has psychological benefits in private, to do with her personality. There is a nemesis, a large man, in the room down the corridor from her own cubicle, large physically and intellectually, who deems Melissa *de trop*, who finds her large wooden necklace beading an affront to his bluff grasp of the nature of the universe. So you see that in this state I am the one who is scarred, under imagistic lesions, while she, Melissa, enrols me into her titanic struggle agin the office monster – as if she cares for me, which she does not.

As it is, the offices run down and off a long corridor towards the top of a tall building. Occasionally in my signature slope to work I take the time to scan the roof and find there people, workers surely, keeping all in order for the forty-five storeys beneath their feet. It has to be imagined that they push the physical materials for spiritual well-being down through the tubes and vents and aerials that mark the building's celestial features. At one end of the corridor there are

9

stairs, forbidden, which take you outside and ascend to the summit, if any timid paper pusher or overbearing manager would dare enter the clouds. To my knowledge, there has been no breach, and keeping inside this line has meant that the city has remained in good order. Sometimes the plumbing fails and we suffer under the reek of sewage, along with the nearby train station and shops, and sometimes the alarm goes off and we trundle away from the lifts down endless flights entering the growing stream of doubt. These are not common events, really, not common. And Melissa comes and goes as she pleases into her cubicle, she is all that I perceive. It is possible she should be at work, at her desk, more often. The system is lax, and yet, paradoxically, it is in good order.

II

I see Melissa handed down from the carriage, certain that in me is a man who is fascinated by the woman he knows at work and who he comes into contact with only tangentially. There is nothing romantic or erotic in this dynamic with the woman, just the intrigue of another life which he has no access to and which he has to constantly extrapolate from, often from small scraps. He fortuitously comes across a letter she has torn and thrown away and is faced with a moral dilemma. He reads it, but it reveals nothing but some mundanities about officialdom. The family, in her name, it is addressed to her, is behind in payments for groceries, an unusual arrangement. A shame comes over me, not because with so little struggle I took out the letter which promised so much and gave so little, but a shame that I didn't wrestle with a conscience regarding her privacy, this unwarranted and unknowable to her intrusion into the life of herself and familiars.

III

The fear is a more unknown woman much further down the corridor, who carries the sign on her face. Melissa's scar is ordinary, misplaced, accidental, stable. Her name could be anything, I haven't discovered it and it has not been unconcealed, as if it is one of those names which cannot be spoken for fear of invoking demons. All misogynistic folk nonsense, obviously, as I watch the scar dance over her face under a difficult light – the new lights, as all things, supposedly an improvement on the old ways, and sometimes they are, and many times we are disappointed. The fear which grips is straight out of Poe, a childhood favourite author, that the scar on this unknown woman is the outward sign of some inner moral imperfection which does not exist other than in my projection on to her. Am I one of those terrible Poe Men? I believe not. The work I am obliged to do is tedious, a Kafka Clerk am I caught in the bureaucratic machine with nothing, not even a modern mind. Melissa is handed down from the carriage in the nearby station, leaving a letter behind for me to read, as if she didn't know. Where had she been to return so late on a Sunday evening, unencumbered by children, in typical harassed, *distrait* mode. Melissa! The letter is a bill for unpaid groceries, a fabrication – nobody has a personal grocer from whom vegetables are obtained on the never-never.

IV

The tedium of my work, my failure to exist, was illustrated this morning when I came in early to complete online fire awareness training. To ensure I passed the test this time I made notes on the various extinguishers and the different kinds of fire they came with and the colour codes that would mean survival for the block. Tomorrow I will have forgotten. Nevertheless, so that this is not wasted time it is possible to think that tomorrow if there is a fire alarm, on the way down the stairs I can start a conversation around the theme of fire and discover what others know and remember. There was a fire alarm once and somebody panicked, unusually. It's not very often, either, that you see pictures of people scarred in fires, from wars. Another childhood memory is the scene in the film *Great Expectations* when Miss Haversham's wedding dress catches fire. I tremble now.

V

The effort to unravel the mystery of the mysterious woman is some days too great. Because I had come into work so early, so alone, this morning, by mid-afternoon I would not have surprised myself if I had fallen asleep, nap-style, lacking the energy to bring to mind the mystery woman. When I was thinking this Melissa came in. One of the dangerous things about Melissa, one of the great things, is her lack of respect for authority, not lack of respect so much, rather the lack of fear in telling everybody what she thinks and going straight to the top when necessary and not through the necessary recommended channels. She had a light brown motif enlivened by patches of purple in a neck veil and oversized material handbag, and says 'you're not the boss of me' to somebody in the office. Her husband is a musician, plays viola for the City orchestra. Beyond that, he is an uninteresting mystery, and perhaps seen as such by Melissa, for it is well-known to me that for five years her love is outside marriage, with the family's agreement. Melissa is the boss of her soul. The scar, then, if it is to mean anything, must mean this shiny tissue of spirit that is Melissa. Having understood that, having returned something to her in the way of speech before she leaves us or me, the fascination falls into desuetude for the remainder of the week.

VI

There is a thin veil between me and the city. The shadowy figures are not just at the far end of the corridor, in a building that houses a small city, they are everywhere, seeking out other shadows, other living wraiths. Their arms do not move in silhouette, dark shapes leaning out of doorways, half-free from the machine. As to Melissa's whereabouts outside the building, we now have the clue of the grocery store, about a mile from my own place. As if the planets are suddenly in alignment, today is the day I make *Parmigiana* for which I require six aubergines.

The image of her descent from the carriage, bearing the scar. I make my way to a seat, not realising it had been her seat, still warm (everybody rushed on, heading for Leeds and beyond), rummaging my poor noggin for any reason why she should be getting off a long-distance train from Penzance, totally alone, bearing the unrelated scar. I pick up the rubbish somebody has left behind, very annoyed at the rail company and the person with slovenly habits. There is a crumpled large polystyrene cardboard cup, an envelope, a half-eaten pie. All on the seat. The company has dispensed with bins. The rubbish goes underneath the seat as I glance at the address and am jolted out of my turpitude (off to some performance of *Lear*, headed off, out of duty, half-wondering why I have proposed to marry Inga on the floor below. She bears nothing). There are no mirrors on these trains, never have been, and I would want to see the look on my face when I apprehended the import of what I held in my hands: the life of Melissa.

VII

Decidedly effortless with Inga's family, decidedly. The day went well and here we are, installed. I try not to think of Melissa's life.

VIII

I woke earlyish, about 6.45, had a shave. Inga didn't want a coffee and barely spoke, so I got on with my own morning, the television, that thought about death, sitting in traffic, waiting, full of sloth. Would she be there? All I had was the grocery store bill, and that was now receding for her as it stayed live for me. The thought about being in the lift with the others from the other floors. We were not all in the same business, we were not all thinking about Melissa's life. If Melissa had a scar and an aubergine? The lift opened and Melissa walked past without vegetables and I got out and walked in the other direction. Was Inga sick? Wouldn't she go to work? Since our wedding day there was little motivation for her to come to work and my thoughts turned to being with Inga at home. Why work? What was the point? Perhaps the whole point of work had been a confluence with Melissa, whose life remained unattainable, and once realised, I should now cease working, I should cease producing, I should be more like Inga. Melissa had more purpose than ever, and this was not to be borne by the slothful ones. Really, no, really, what was the point? Do not work! I put up the sign, the symbol of the newfound lassitude, this paradoxical infusion of excitement at the possibility of being at home with the wife and doing fuck all. We should get to know each other in a way we hadn't already, since we had signed up to be in each other's life. It was just not possible to be in Melissa's life, I could only do it with Inga. The gift of the *aperçu* had produced nothing beyond the initial *frisson*, and I was left *frissonless*. Fooking frissonless. The very thought of it enraged me, it was all Melissa's fault (I saw Melissa get into the lift with a handbag with a broken strap, carrying it like a sick animal, and my heart went out to her, broken, it was all broken, the whole of life, hers, mine, Inga's).

IX

How could I turn winter into summer? How could I escape the triangular *impasse* in which our lives had turned to an accumulation of dead tissue, a natural wasteland, a final global cicatrice. There was nothing for it but to bring together my beloved and my Inga, to go from pique to peak and back again, refreshed by weird pulchritude. To which end I turned to the cream porcelain box full of tiny white lies, and, in vulgar parlance, 'hatched a scheme', whereby the two women would be in the same place at the same time. I would be unobserved, in disguise, bedazzled by the conjunction of Melissa-Inga, two singular people to be enmeshed by grace and gravity, all to aid the purposive thrill-seeking of elective affinities.

The past few months had made me realise that vegetables held no special place in Melissa's lived world, parmigiana or no, and that only meat-rich delicacies released the spring of her imagination. The city had refused to yield up duck tongue pate to her palate, either not having heard of it or there not being enough ducks, and she had not the time to make the starter herself (so a handful of spies confirmed to me), an absence no doubt feeding her city chafe (I live in constant dread lest she move to a better place, of which, I am sure, there are many).

Inga's fake identity sent a café rendezvous invite. (The alternative from the box of white lies would be to embroil Inga and Melissa in some spurious office politics involving the office monster, perhaps to do with the ambivalence of reconstruction). Fake Inga's message read: 'Hi Melisa. Somebody in the office said youd kill for duck tongue pattay. Everybodys talking about itandIknow where to get some. See you atMonks tomorrow, three. Ingaxxx'. God bless the

14

fake Inga, for it worked: 'Amazing, Inga – where did you get it? Until tomorrow!!! Melissa x'. Melissa's openness to experience and people, the lack of suspicion, these were new characteristics of Melissa revealed, just when I thought all joy had been exhausted. Three exclamation marks – so unexpected, yet so *right*. Or perhaps the times we live in demand an inflation of declaratives. (There were further workaday exchanges between fake Inga and real Melissa describing how they would recognize each other – fake Inga's self-portrait was overly modest. Such practicalities have no place here. Should I confess how much I enjoy playing fake Inga, to this day, or is it obvious?)

The ormolu sun rose in good spirits the next day, as if raised on my delicate laurels, and to complete the plan I arranged to meet my wife, the real Inga, at Monks at three. She had no other plans for the afternoon, for Inga, once so disciplined, had ascended to sublime, slatternly habits.

The hours in my office that day consisted of gargantuan seconds clunking along in sequence, until the time came for me to change into a disguise (which I cannot divulge in case I need to re-use) allowing me to follow Melissa from the office to Monks, diving into shop doors and doing up my shoelaces when in danger of being spotted. I knew the promise of duck tongue pate would not prevent Melissa from being late (another charming feature), nor from her wearing an unfortunate red woollen hat which she favoured, perched half-way back on the skull. When we arrived at the café I took a seat outside, faced in, odd as it may have seemed to others, and watched the real Melissa take off her hat and search for my real Inga. (Inga had already texted me asking where I was. I said I was running late.) Just to reiterate: inside Monks Inga looked for me and Melissa looked for Inga. Melissa introduced herself to Inga, and Inga, a frown now to be scored permanently across her shiny brow, seeing as how I was nowhere to be seen (in reality only a few pleasing feet away, separated by the miracle of an expanse of plate glass, the angelic demarcation of externality and interior, was I really on the outside?), she realized that fate had thrust the wayward Melissa into her life, and looked inwardly pleased she had been duped into some new role by her new husband. He had played a trick she would never forgive, yet she may at that moment have understood that at last, it was I who was in the wrong, and could not be healed.

Correspondence

At the word 'ptarmigan' Franz groaned outwardly. The others seemed to understand so Franz said nothing and let the afternoon drag on. What made it worse was he couldn't remember the context or the sentence. His brain wouldn't let it go at all and for around four hours generated possible phrases. 'We will meet ptarmigan once more'. 'We should stand up to the egregious ptarmigan'. 'There is no alternative. It is ptarmigan. Or bust. Colleagues'.

Outside the building it was still sweltering. He took the tram to Petrin Hill, trying hard not to look at the men with large, unwashed ears, who by the look of their clothes came from the outlying villages. When he turned away from them he saw women with dirty necks and hard stares. He tried to focus on nothing, which only served to let ptarmigan back in. 'There is more ptarmigan on the trams than ever before'. The Manager took every opportunity to disparage public transport.

In the park, walking up the hill, there were some children with elemental wooden toy rifles. Three of the boys were blindfolded, queuing up for the firing squad. 'Josef first' shouted a girl who was older than the others. One of the boys was guided to the nearest tree and placed with his back against it. Four children took aim.

'Josef, you are a traitor. Fire'.

The guns made a popping sound and Josef fell to the floor in a realistic heap, blood bursting over his shirt. It was the same for the second boy, who collapsed onto the first. The boy beneath didn't flinch. Franz wondered if he should intervene, but he was anxious they might pretend to turn on him. Also, he wanted a story to tell Charlotte, who he knew was drawn to the darker side of childhood. The girl, who they called 'Katrina' or 'Kat', ordered

16

the third boy to stand ready for the firing squad. 'Josef. You make no sense to us. Fire'. The newly-executed boy made a point of jumping on top of the first two. Franz moved on. After ten minutes, walking and sweating, he looked back and could just make the group out from between the trees. Two of the dead boys hadn't moved. They were very good, he thought. He couldn't have stayed still that long. 'Ptarmigan, yes'. Beyond the children the city was a sunny, hazed picture, and he was glad he lived there.

Back in the house there was no meat. He made himself a vegetable stew. While it was simmering he sat down to write to Charlotte.

Dear, dear Charlotte. Is it true some of your teeth are missing? I read in your letters of trips to the dentist. Is there anaesthetic? I know your father is a believer and has promoted the cause.

Your eyes, Charlotte, your grey, penetrating eyes, divine my soul.

All the best.

F.

There was not the passion, he knew, to arouse her. He would write a better one, more fiery, after tea, if Max didn't show. He was determined to win Charlotte's affection.

***

Leni passed her hand over Franz's bare back, slowly transforming the palm of her hand into a finger and then to a nail when it reached the beginning of the long, dark cleft. It was then she knew it was time to end their fitful liaisons. 'Franz's bottom is gloomy' she thought, 'Henri's isn't. I'm finished with Franz'.

'I have a game', she said. 'Hey, Franz, I have a game!'

'Yes?'

'I will write on your back with my finger, and you tell me the word'.

'Okey dokey'.

She traced out the letter 'F'. He complained it was a letter, not a word. She spelt out his first name, which he guessed correctly. Then she spelt out her name, which he guessed correctly. Then she wet her finger and casually scrawled 'fine', starting at the neck's nape and ending at the base of the spine.

'Fine', he said, 'everything's fine. Franz. Leni. Fine'.

'No', she said, 'it isn't'. She wrote it out again on his back this time cutting the letters into his flesh with the nail of her right forefinger, which she had sharpened in advance. He didn't flinch. She told him of her cruelty, lest he become anxious about her behavior, and said she spoke Italian. When she finished the last stroke of the letter 'e' he understood and pronounced the word as she intended.

***

On his way back he encountered the good Doctor on one of his life-saving errands, a hinged black leather bag in one hand and clutched in the other the same book that Franz was reading.

'What a book!', said Franz, 'what a book!'

'The man is a great psychologist, our first, a doctor even', shouted the Doctor. He had whiskers which Franz had once tried to imitate, like the Englishmen whom they both admired. 'Fear . . . and trembling', shouted the good Doctor. 'That's it. That's everything!'

'Yes!', agreed Franz, laughing. 'And we must sacrifice our sons!'

'It's against the law!'

'Pah! Who cares for our laws!?'

The good Doctor, through his whiskers, sensed something wrong.

'What is it Franz?'

'My back, doc, festers like a ptarmigan. I don't know. Bye'.

***

There was another meeting at work, first thing in the morning. It was limited to the insurance clerks. 'Capercaillie', said the Manager, amongst other things.

'How are we spelling that, Sir?', asked Tomas, who was new.

Franz groaned outwardly, for he knew the Manager would never tell them, and there was no ready means of finding out. Eight hours trying to spell 'capercaillie', on top of the rest of his work.

***

18

The hot days continued. Franz made his way up the hill, tracing the steps he'd laid down yesterday and the days before, frequently stopping to look back out and across his city. Half way up, as usual, two of the boys were playing dead and Katrina intoned a lament over the bodies. It sounded like she had just learned the word 'perfidy' for she kept stuttering over it. He wished the boys would show some signs of life. Franz wanted to put his foot under one of the bodies and casually flip it over. Katrina saw Franz watching and he moved on.

There were three bits of boiled beef he had picked up from Max's on his way home, and he threw these into the remains of the vegetable stew. While it was cooking on a low, gentle heat he composed another letter to Charlotte.

Dear Charlotte,

My body aches and bleeds for you. There is a hunger in me that only your letters can satiate. What is this world, without the knitting together of hearts? Your father must release you. Shall I come to your rescue? On a white steed?

I see your grey, penetrating eyes, slaking my soul.

Without you I die a thousand deaths ~~every day~~ in this wonderful city every day.

F.

He thought how small Charlotte was, and how plain, ugly even, and how the tiny, dull frame contained a volcano. Was that enough for Franz? Was it truly enough to transcend the physical? He couldn't live in doubt. What if he was wrong, and all this time it wasn't Charlotte but Leni his heart desired? Charlotte would disapprove of his dissolute lifestyle, he knew that, and might turn him down because of it. 'That's why the first letter is so important to get right', he muttered. The doubt ruined his appetite. In disgust at himself he took the stew from the heat and put it in a bowl for the dog, whose tongue burned and burned and burned until he had no choice but to turn it out of doors into the narrow streets.

***

Max visited the next night after work. Franz gave him his own supper, not feeling hungry.

'Which way did you come?'

'Up the hill'.

'Did you see the dead boys?'

'No. I would have noted and remembered. . . . You're getting thin again. Who is it this time?'

'Leni has finished with me. Charlotte refuses to write'.

Capercaillie, Franz thought. Perhaps the Manager, the shallowest of all men, is wise. If only he could get the courage to ask him. Ptarmigan. When would it end?

***

The Doc told Franz there might be a cholera outbreak in their beautiful city. He had already attended two cases which had ended badly.

'Leave the city, my friend'. He groomed his whiskers in earnest.

'The city is beautiful. If it dies, I must die'.

'Don't talk nonsense'.

'I have seen two dead boys'.

***

At work he looks for signs of cholera in the other clerks. But they fear nothing, and show no signs. Franz groans outwardly. The Manager calls him into his office. 'Fine siskins . . .' The Manager has a habit of dropping his voice after the first few words in a sentence. Franz senses something is changing.

'Siskins, Sir?'

'Yes. Take Carla to the ballet'. Carla is the Manager's niece. "C" loves the ballet'.

'Which one is it?'

The Manager tells him. 'Do you know it?'

'Partly'. From nowhere comes courage. 'Sir, these words you use, unfamiliar words which I don't understand, words such as'

'That's all Franz. Enjoy the ballet. Here, this should pay for the evening. Have dinner on me as well. You must eat, my boy. Eat! You are too thin!'

20

Dear Ellen,

The strangest thing – strange strange – I have received a letter – written in German. John Greewood, my bookseller brought it to Martha when Father was out on Parish business. He collected it from a friend of his in Keighley. It is signed 'F'. John says it must stand in for 'Fritz' but I think 'Frederick'. You don't read German, so I have translated freely for you on the enclosed sheet. He tells me I am small, and plain, ugly even. This is admirable truth – I like him all the better for it. But is it a declaration of love? Can we call it a love letter? He says he burns for me. I am on his mind always so much he cannot eat. I have known this starvation of the spirit – Ellen – do you remember? Our religious crisis? He says he is not well, and describes 'yellow siskins', a German disease that scars the back of the body. The place? The city he says is beautiful, deadly, full of ghosts, boys dying, churches, cholera. He writes stories and asks me if I would like to read them. I have sent a note back via John and his friend in Keighley who has F's secret address telling him it is improper. His letter is beautifully written. I have wrapped it in oiled silk, sealed it in a stoppered glass, and buried it. The arrangements are those made by our heroic explorers of the Arctic for preservation of their diaries and journals, I tell you, when they know they are without hope and are about to die. I buried his letter beneath the nearest tree when father was out on Parish business, but I would prefer to bury it under ice. I don't believe *The Times*. Men would never eat each other – under any circumstance – definitely not Shackleton's men.

You should burn this letter. Not the others – we agreed. My letters are worthless ephemera.

Yours with affection

Charles Thunder.

P.S. He says each day he is executed. The girl, Katrina, kicks his body down the hill. Each day he wakes at the bottom of the hill and the children stand over him, laugh, and disperse. He crawls back home and dresses for work, but is frightened of the Manager, so he devotes his time to looking for Katrina. At first he reasoned that the whole city must pass over the bridge that bears my name (which city is this, Ellen?) so he waits there for Katrina, for weeks, eating nothing, crawling home, or carried back to Max's house. Each absence from the bridge makes him anxious and means he must start again.

Ellen, I omitted from the translation, and write now here in my Postscript what he writes in his – What do you know of passion, my darling Charlotte? The passion of the body? – then he describes his body, all the way down to an elongated, dingy crevasse, the back above seared by my 'attentions'. I translate the word as 'attentions'. The word he uses I think is improper, disgusting, the worst German gutturality I suspect, chosen to shock me. I can not ask my friends what the word signifies, for then my friends will know how a man I have not been introduced to writes to me. I imagine he wishes to say that he bears the arrows of Saint Sebastian. That is how <u>he</u> used to glorify himself when he was not well.

***

'Max! Look at this letter. From Charlotte! At last!!!'

***

Kat's mother and father were fighting. Kat shouted 'bye' and dragged her sister Clara out. 'My school bag', she groaned. 'Kat, you've left my bag in the house!'
    'You don't need it. We have to meet Franz'.
    'Let me go, Kat'.
    'Let's hide from Franz instead'.

***

max promise me you will destroy everything
except charlotte's letter to
burn m

The Whale of Penlan Tork

On the Air

We climbed the poles to discuss the whale of Penlan Tork, recently discovered off the coast of Patagonia, languishing in kelp forests.

    Chorus: O mighty pillars!
    Simon: Welcome.

The shadow government settled itself into the lotus position, curious. Across the tops of minarets and church steeples they thought they could make out sailing ships and the horizon, make out the sun's descent from the heavens. There was a dutiful wish that all they saw and thought would blend into one, sky, windows, ocean, prayers. We asked Simon what he knew of the journey to Patagonia. The saint mapped a route to the lower part of the globe along the third Christian highway – here you would be taken in by the Order of Beppo, there the hospitality would be from the House of Alessius, here there was some dispute amongst the brethren over Deuteronomy, and in the next port you would find a codification of Jewish slavery laws agreed by disparate Hebraic fellows.

    Simon: Our minds are open. The chosen will set sail from Devonport.
    Chorus: O mighty pillars!

Was the test Simon's for us? Was the test the traditional one, to remain with Simon on the pillars working in the shadow of the usurpers, who had been there since 425, or to understand Tork's legacy?

23

Simon: Who will travel from Devonport to Patagonia?

Chorus: What's the purpose?

Simon: A quest!

Chorus: Yes, but for what?

Simon: The whale of Penlan Tork.

Chorus: We have no authority.

Simon: Perhaps we need the approval of the Government, perhaps not. Who is to say?

Azure blackens. There is no resolution. Staying on the pillars is everything. We know this, and yet we cannot match Simon's dedication, so we go inside the pillars to the poles, descend and return home, redundant firemen. It occurs to us that anyone who embarks on the journey will need a commitment as great as Simon's, yet if we cannot even remain on the pillars for months, let alone years, as Simon has shown the way, how can any one of us make the journey to the Patagonian kelp forests. Our geography is poor, our knowledge of the natural world is poor, our understanding of Tork's legacy is slight. It is not helped by Simon using his own names for places. We have discovered that one of the names he uses refers to the island of St Jago, and another to Bahia in the Brazils, but on this projection of discovery it would take decades to decode or translate Simon's world into ours. Yet we know we must persevere: Devonport, St Jago, Bahia. These are real and provide reference points of sorts, dots on the surface to be joined by the ones who voyage South. Or is it East?

Our noses bleed. Another test.

Back on the pillars, bloodied rags in hand, we seek to comfort each other and to vie with each other for Simon's good opinion. He will observe the strength of our nose bleeds, the tickle with grass in the nostrils. Is this how Simon will choose? We think it is.

Chorus: Simon, do we need to know Tork's legacy? Should we mention the others from history, like J . . .

Simon: No! No mention of others, only Tork. Yes, you should know his legacy. No, it will not help to know this.

Chorus: But when we meet the whale of Penlan Tork and speak, what do we need to know?

Simon: I am no oracle, I cannot say in advance. One thing I will say: this is the *Whale* of Penlan Tork, it is *not Penlan Tork*. No one shall know Penlan Tork.

It's not great when Simon adopts the oracular tone, it strikes a note which we are suspicious of. It is the false Simon that emerges sometimes. We attempt to clean our noses. Simon has not noticed the way we cheat our way into his good books by using the special grass to make our noses bleed.

The Voyage

Simon did away with all formalities, chose a group of fortunates at random, the strength of our nose bleeds had no bearing on the decision, and we set sail from Devonport. There are six of us – me, Gary, Martin, Pag, HH, qjd8f-yllll* – plus the sailors manning the ship. We were the entire Chorus. Simon is alone. Gary thinks the masts are like the platforms we've left behind.

Gary: O! Mighty pillars.

In the uncertain weather Gary's tight curly black hair and stock body and face are animated, and he is in his forties. Of all of us he was the least committed to staying on the pillars, finding neither joy within nor without, and so his choice for the voyage quest proves the randomness of Simon. Gary mentions something about the lack of women, for he has a lusty appetite, he says.

The sailors overhear him and a delegate forbids him to mention women, they are bad luck at sea. Some of us have wives and sweethearts back home, which makes it difficult for us to stay on the pillars or to come away, so we are not happy with this reminder. Martin tells him cessation. I like Martin, all redness – hair, face, attitude, in his thirties – and would like to say the things he says, not just think them, and would like to be him, keeping a bit of who I am. Simon has given us no clues as to how to cope with the women missing from our lives, or the women we will encounter on our travels.

Gary: Sirens!

The sailors tell him to get real and we descend to our shockingly cramped cabins. I still have not mastered the hammock, I am useless at sea and throw up all the time. As much as I stand next to The Great Red One nothing changes me, I am useless, his character does not rub off on me and if anything anxiety increases the closer we move to the Equator. Martin leaps into his hammock while I struggle. It was easier to ascend the poles and stay on the platforms and now it is dawning on me that we are ill-prepared for the voyage and ill-prepared to meet the whale, and begin to blame Simon. Although I expressed my worry earlier on that we wouldn't know how to deal with the peculiar cetacean when we were face-to-face it hasn't sunk in to any of the others and still we press ahead towards the Equator as if all is well.

The immediate worry is the heat. We are approaching the Equator, and the sailors have indicated that there are rituals to be observed when we cross it. Coupled with the heat, which isn't too bad at the minute, and the horror of Equator rituals, my anxiety increases, and I still haven't found my sea-legs, and the other five have found theirs. Gary is surprisingly adept at being on the ship and ascends the masts for fun, from the crow's nest staring into the sun with hooded eyes to where sea and sky join forces. There is a fascination for the natural world in him so that he could be possessed by Darwin's ghost, or perhaps he sees himself as Captain Fitzroy, he does like to talk about the weather and is often right in his forecasts. Or perhaps he's just Gary, and we should leave it at that, at his own estimation, the black-haired one, travelling down to Rio.

Days in to the journey and I am still helped into my hammock like a small child. It seems incredible that I was able to ascend a pole to the platform. I wonder how Simon is faring without us.

To mark crossing the Equator the sailors . . . called it 'Neptunes' . . . had learnt that we came from pillars, ascended and descended poles . . . for their fun, used this information, made us . . . now we know they do not respect us . . . must persist 'until we reach the whale of Penlan Tork', which is now our song . . . have mastered the hammock but am unable to walk or sit . . . the hammock is my refuge. Pag and the others seem unaffected. It can only be me.

My Report.
Dear Sirs,
Here is the elemental voyage: *heat; indolence; lassitude; abundance of flora and fauna; the tropics; quarterdeck; homesickness/revolting/slavery; pockets full of 'sins, sins'; sounding the depths; fathoms; anchored for the night; islands/rocks/insects/ plants; midshipmen; quarter master; flying fish on deck; a crab sticking to a fish causing it indescribable pain; wrecks; Commanding Officer; having to kill the poultry with stones for dinner; exhaustion/fatigue/hunger; mandeika/cassada – a food, but can also produce a poison; effect of walking on mimosa;* 'Returned by the old route to Campos Novos; the ride was very tiresome, passing over a heavy & scorching sand. Chirping sand' – according to Darwin, who shadows us - what's 'chirping sand', Charles, what?*; foremast; main shrouds and forestay; Admiral; cutlasses; high and violent surf; pass ports; men dressed in white – a flock of wild fowl;* 'The Admiral sung out "A Raking shot has cut our fore-shrouds". This was only pretend though, in preparation for a real war. There is no devil in this land' and Darwin has departed once more. We are on our own.
End of My Report

After the equator and the Brazils it starts to get cold, and we worry about frozen wastes and the feeling of home.

Simon, Alone

Was I wrong to reject the chance to rule, albeit with conditions? On reflection, I am never wrong. The joint ownership of power would have left me entangled in the thickets of bus pass legislation with no perceptible improvement in the people's lot. This is not why I believe in power. For Simon it is all or nothing. I would rather be on high in the wild air than trapped into a power-sharing arrangement in which my credibility, built up over decades of platform intransigence, remains solid. Now that the six of my Attylites have departed and my experiment with a shadow oligarchy has failed I return to Simon.

As soon as the six leave Simon realises the awful truth that he prefers to be in the shadow government to actual government and his ideas for ruling the country have become ever more fantastic and removed from reality. As Simon predicted to himself on many occasions, as more and more climbed the poles to reach him, as the shadow oligarchy of two or three became less focussed, and as more ideas came into his head than could be dealt with in any single day or given period, until there were the six on the poles and he had his favourites, he liked being the head of a shadow government that could monitor the doings of the government and suggest better policies and strategies for the ideal world. He became ever more fantastic in following through his own shadow agenda, since the trajectories of both governments, close enough in the beginning, had diverged more and more widely. What started out as plausible virtuality had now to be considered as twisted and wholly untoward. The new advantage lay in a hinterland perfection of flaws as execution of the real world repeatedly found itself nosed up against wrinkles, lumps, lacunae, bolts from the blue, unforeseen circumstances and inexplicable happenings which no amount of legislation and policy initiatives could apprehend. Inertia, misplaced sentiment and downright idiocy ensured that everything carried on and those in their everyday habitations noticed little change, or big changes crept up on them which they unknowingly assimilated, providing the occasion for a wry smile. Simon's world was self-sustaining in its rightness. Predicted erreoneosity could be turned to advantage or slain, and Simon was all-powerful in this realm. Infrastructure, the public sector, health care, jobs, foreign policy, nothing discomposed Simon's gathering of the well-meaning. Himself, governance, thought shapes, all firm and fair. Oligarchy dished out the just desserts.

At what cost? The incumbents point to shaky calculations, and it is true, economics is not Simon's strong point. There are gaps that I cannot plug. I have tried. The mystic qjd8f-yllll* has been enlisted to plug away and offer a more credible economic policy. He talks of deep space, the sound of 'om', the pervasive universal consciousness.

And now I understand what is required is a risky change to more sober modelling. The shadow government must be allowed to rule *as a shadow government* with the full authority of the 'real' government. Only when the Ideal Form takes hold in the real way will true progress in all spheres be effected. This I authentically believe. The question remains in rigorous analysis, does such a radical break with previous models of governance require permission from the current government, or can I (we?) enact usurpation? Perhaps, perhaps not, I remain anxious and undecided. If the six return from Patagonia, successful or not, I will tell them to prepare for government in no uncertain terms. This is what qjd8f-yllll* has divined. I will tell them that shadows can work, for there is no shadow without substance, we are both substance and shadow, real and ideal. The proper government shines no light on itself, has no complement, we are our own created shadows, we are not the property and function of the proper government. I hate the proper government. It has done nothing but use blunt instruments – design, science, manufacture, a Gradgrindean education – and has left the purity of abstraction to rot with me. I await the return of the six and will move on from there.

What if qjd8f-yllll* is wrong? The others, Pag included, have full credentials. qjd8f-yllll* has cast some kind of spell on me I am sure. It is to be hoped that he is good at heart and will prove a constant friend to the others on the voyage. This is devoutly to be wished.

Simon: O! Chorus. Help!

Pag, sycophant to the last, is the one I miss most.

Simon: qjd8f-yllll*! Should I abandon you? Will you abandon me?

I am of a mind now to attempt an assault on the government without either the permission of the government, and, what has no precedent, the support of the six. Is this rash, after decades of patience? Fah! Patience for what? I am at the end of my patience, sat up here, looking out onto the emptiness of platforms, flat mundane roofs and roofs shaped to religious design. Simon meditates. So much to bring into the one – the others, myself, the voyage, ideas about government, the lids on the tops of buildings, inside the buildings, my Ideals battling against Real objects and against ideas which are made reality.

qjd8f-yllll* has taught me how to properly meditate. Before I allowed him on board I meditated in an amateurishly intense way to make solid all my perceptions of the world. qjd8f-yllll* has shown me how to combine perceptions of the world, the shadow government, Ideal, and me, into one. Perhaps I was a bad student for even now I cannot make all these things coalesce, I cannot make all these things me. I blame qjd8f-yllll* at the end of each day, it is my mantra, and that is why I banned him with good reason, although inside there are qualms, I confess.

When my hatred for qjd8f-yllll* rises I calm myself with the image of Pag, rotund Pag, deferential, telling me of my greatness, his derisory beard. He is good to hear and reassures. Sometimes, looking back, Pag's boosts to my ego were what most kept Simon going.

Azure blackens. Tomorrow the government will make more overtures to me, will want to use my credibility to give credibility to some new fiscal measures which will prove unpopular. I have told them that if they can make their way up the poles I will parlay and replace the fiscal with the monetary, leading them up the garden path of their own limited understanding. My answer at the end of each day must always then be 'no. Return to year zero. Things with intrinsic value. Things in themselves. No mediated equivalences'. I thank qjd8f-yllll* for this insight.

**

It was a surprise, the gentle questions about the whale of Penlan Tork, the attempt on the part of this government to talk about nothing else with me. In other circumstances this would have been absolutely fine, and we could have chatted about it over dinner or cocktails, or whatever passes for politeness these days, I am so out of touch being so pure of spirit. Yes, we could have discussed the creature and possible connections with the history of popular music. I would have disowned the idea that I have any specialist knowledge and would talk merely as an enthusiast. I could not see what the government wanted out of me. I raised the issue of usurpation, shooting myself in the foot, and the issue of recombination of all that there is in the world inside each of our heads, for the good of all, and explained my Ideal economy of things in themselves, all to no avail. They would speak of nothing except the whale of Penlan Tork, and I can do nothing except remember that qjd8f-yllll* had predicted just such a scenario. I needed Pag, his oleaginous puffing of Simon, for I indeed then would have had more courage. It reminded me of the time when I had attempted to persuade the government to Reform, to allow only those with a concern in the country to vote. Idlers have no investment in the common wealth so I do not see that they should have a say in the running of the common wealth. Pag approved; qjd8f-yllll* attempted to dissuade; the government rudely declined to consider a change in voting regulations. Even if I am resigned to remaining in the Shadow Government, which I am very far from doing, that I can command a nation is everything, and I can do everything for them. Hang on . . . the Sky is on Fire; a terrible storm interrupts my thoughts of Reform with the plasma of a million candles shaped into a great red moving ball in the heavens; the shocking light dazzles from the steeples and minarets, burnishes them, strikes the souls at the back of my eyes.

Pag did agree with me before he left, rounder than ever, as if the slope of his belly was casting his head backwards and making that slope too, much too big for a man in his mid-thirties, very pleasant, amiable, and awe-struck, that despotism was clearly more attractive than the cancer of democracy where nothing changed and the poor stayed poor and the rich stayed rich, or, let's face it, the promise of oligarchy. Pag agreed that I would make a good despot. I nodded in agreement. qjd8f-yllll* shook his head slowly and urged me to meditate, where I would find the impossibility of integrating despotism with all the aforementioned items that constitute the universe. 'Every thing is everything' he said, 'and *that* is democratic. A despot always becomes despotic, not more benign. Why not a theocracy?'. At last, at last! qjd8f-yllll*'s persuasion had stumbled blinking into our world. And so, for Simon, never had despotism looked so attractive in the face of such nonsense. 'Democracy discriminates against the minority', I said, 'to no good effect. Only a despot can ensure consistency and fairness'. In this I am right. Hence, I have sent off the others to experience a ship and a whale of note.

The Whale

The chorus concluded that the whale of Penlan Tork had chosen the kelp forests off Patagonia so that it could rest without effort – the kelp formed an interesting bed. There was no communication between the chorus and the whale, unless the whale was to sing on frequencies we could not hear. It is possible said Pag that he talks to Simon and no-one else, that at this minute he is relaying back information about us. Pag was downcast at his usurpation. Either the whale of Penlan Tork is not what it seems, or it is all that it seems.

Is it that the whale was content, had fulfilled its early promise as a young whale? Or is it, was it, by resting in thickets of kelp, slowly finding a pleasurable death?

The whale had ably disentangled itself from all social contact, obsessed with the generation of music use that can only be derived from long, thin metal strips, like typewriter letter-arms elongated to five or six feet, and each one a full note representation in itself, no, not a note only, a full harmony extended beyond an untempered thirteenth. This was the secret of a musical success, finally, and the whale can communicate it around the sea-globe in some approximation to the music it imagined creating.

The one man who would understand all this was Penlan Tork, a whale from way back.

qjd8f-yllll* heard the whale speak in what is the background pop harmony of Penlan Tork, saying 'qjd8f-yllll*'s shadow has mastered the unwieldy long thin metal harmony strips singing to qjd8f-yllll*'.

The whale of Penlan Tork bore no resemblance to anything yet encountered, a counterbalance of blades and bladders. Beneath us the reef will still not yield its elongated metal harmony strips. Our elongated musical lives can only echo or shadow the original depth. I wanted to ask the whale about Berlin before reunification.

The Career of the Idea of Penlan Tork

Our sixed-out whale falls to the bottom of the ocean, dying downwards, each packet of memory quantum dying per foot descent. It will take a hundred years for blades the size of sheet metal to pass themselves on to the blades below. The sea-otters nuzzle Penlan and take in some of his ideas about nutrients, for the whale is not yet decomposed to nutrients. Yet, everything is lost, all greatness is bloated.

Once on the ocean's reef the whale of Penlan Tork can begin decomposition in earnest amongst the kelp holdfasts, can be colonized, can be everything. The idea of Penlan Tork moves forward from the coast of South America. Always the actor, he seeks ballast. Can the idea fuse with the idea? This kelp is named after Penlan and is one-hundred-and-fifty feet long, filled with an ache for new sources of light. The kelp needs this to be photographed from below, above, within, conscious of its largesse in holding whales that avoid killer whales. Can this kelp too be known as great now that the whale of Penlan Tork decomposes? The sea-otters nuzzle Penlan, do not notice Penlan Tork and his vocation.

Teacher Story

One

Absolute quotidian detail but its delivery makes it *unheimlich*. Too obvious? Amidst it all is the story of the students giving the teacher a jumper with glass fragments sewn into the neck. He is under no obligation to wear it, they tell him. 'We know you like jumpers with large collar overturns, and the colour racing green'.

'*British* Racing Green', pipes up Helen.

'There was some dispute!', says Ingar, taking the lead once more.

Rames is the history teacher who is the focus of the story, and the students who feel for him have finished their final exams and are about to leave school forever. They are aware that he has a sad home life, with a wife they call 'fish wife', a type of woman he tells them existed up until the sixteenth century, though not necessarily a wife, a woman who sold fish and was loud-mouthed and coarse. 'So we have made you this jumper. You don't have to wear it. Or you could save it for special occasions like Christmas or your birthday'.

'He doesn't celebrate Christmas'. Rames nods then shakes his head.

'Anyway, Mr Padmore, it's *your* jumper now, a "thank you" from all of us' (there are five of them: Helen, Ingar, Connie, Sanjay and James). Rames takes off his workaday jumper in an awkward fashion and they help him on with the gift jumper, all thinking as he does so that this will make up for his fish wife, if she is a wife, though they've never met her and he's never really spoken about her. The glass shards in the collar begin to make little cuts in his neck. 'Not a good idea to wear all the time, Rames, eh?', suggests James, 'not a good idea *at all*. He touches the teacher's neck with middle and index finger and shows him the blood, 'not . . . a . . . good . . . idea . . .?'

In the story it's important that not too much is made of anything. We don't really get to know the teacher (or do we?). He hates fiction with a vengeance, except Zola, who he regards as a documentary writer in *Germinal*, a novel they won't read. So there is the irony of the story being about a teacher who hates fiction, being in a piece of fiction. What's the point? Entertainment.

Could the story just revolve around Rames (the History Teacher) as a force of attraction so that we get to know the five teenagers about to enter the adult world but don't need to know anything about him? He could be a negative Miss Jean Brodie, since everything we know about him is what they project on to him. His lack of personality is the source of their fascination (they are at an age where personalities are magnified or null, but Rames is in a strange *unheimlich* category of magnified nothingness.)

Once the jumper's been introduced the hyperreal quotidian nature of the story could be foregrounded. He wakes up, making the same promises to himself he makes every morning (the reader isn't told what these promises are). Is there a person next to him? Perhaps the gender is not clear (a cheap trick? – some of the students think he's gay – some of them like this aspect – some don't – it would perhaps parallel for the reader the fascination the students have for him). How to get the tone right.

'He woke up and made the usual promises after the preceding night, as if to orientate himself. The body next to him was breathing deeply. There on the wicker chair at the end of the bed was the jumper the students had given him. Should he wear it today? The students wouldn't be at school any more now they'd finished their final exams. Helen, Ingar, Connie, Sanjay and James. He would remember these students for a long time to come, thanks to the jumper. They said he didn't have to wear it all the time, maybe just special occasions, like his birthday and Christmas and the student ball. He didn't celebrate Christmas, they had forgotten. "It's your favourite colour", Connie said. He was in love with Connie'.

Should the story have this romantic element? Is that what the story is to be about? Would it be possible for a thirty-year-old history teacher with a miserable home-life *not* to fall in love with Connie? She is the sharpest and the funniest. Ingar is the most beautiful (along with Sanjay), but in this particular school the culture that has been encouraged prizes wit above all else. (The story would need to have examples of her wittiness, rather than just saying 'she's incredibly funny', or similar). The problem here is that it starts to lose the *unheimlich* feel. Yet, perhaps *unheimlich* is irrelevant, perhaps it's more just about a slice of life for these eighteen-year olds? Could do it in a *Dubliners* style? No.

Rames looks tenderly at his wife – the early morning sun casts shadows on the voile and picks out the new green jumper. Shona has been suspicious of the gift from the students, the way her husband has carefully avoided saying too much about these particular students, as if hiding his feelings for them. She had spied him with the group of five, as she had intuited, and noticed their animation around her husband. Was he talking history to them? She doubted it. The girls were flirting with him, she could see, she knew. She knew it from her own time at school, and the music teacher she'd had a crush on, and the million-and-one ways she'd found to be in his vicinity, watching him, unable to cope with her own inappropriate feelings. ('Inappropriate feelings'? Nonsense. This needs to go.). She fantasised over Mr Hughes, and could see the attraction the girls had for her man, in general ways, if not for this specific man, her husband.

Rames placed his hand on her bare shoulder, moved by the light through the voile and their earlier fondness for each other. Shona moved away under the touch and out of his easy reach, pretending to shift to a more comfortable position. The small gesture mobilised his heart in a way he hid from himself. The jumper, caught in the light of the early morning sunshine, appeared as some compensation.

Carefully peeling back the sheet so as not to disturb his wife further, Rames wheeled his body round and sat up, facing the window, sideways on to the chair and the jumper. He had yet to try the jumper on properly. Should he wear it? Would that annoy Shona? Shona knew it was a gift from teacher's pets and had made a number of telling, sarky comments. Being at a right-angle to the jumper paralysed him. To look at it would be to betray Shona. Not to look at it would be to give up on . . .

Is this the focus of the story? It's moving away from whatever the heart of it is or was meant to be. It would be better if we had some sense of him thinking about the day ahead. How important is the gift to him? The problem is that without identifying what Rames's character is like, the focus can be pretty much anywhere.

Not to look at it would be to give up on his life, the promise of something more, something transcendental.

Two

The pub after the ball. They go on to a late drinking place and start to drink hard. He's drinking pints with chasers. The students are aware that something has happened at home with his fish wife. They can't get it out of him. The dishevelled clue is that Rames hasn't trimmed his beard. He buys more drinks. If he isn't careful he will become too pathetic for them to care for. Ingar wants to mother him, which he starts to resent. He no longer hides his desire for Connie, and once this starts to happen the dynamics change and the group foresees an inevitable coming together of the two. The excitement of the ball is in the past and everything converges on what will happen with Connie and Rames. ('Too many "happens"' is the comment Rames frequently writes on student history essays).

What to do with Connie now? We don't know Rames, except as a rather agentless creature, yet that is more than we know of Connie's motivations. Why is she sharp? There could be many reasons.

An original(ish) thing to do would be to pick some part of the brain out as being strangely well-developed in Connie, a kind of modern day phrenology using the language of neuroscience which could be the *unheimlich*. I could do that, I think.

Out the window I see the original of Connie. Perhaps that would be better. She lives a couple of doors down in the street opposite mine. I have no idea who she is, or what her name is, except that she looks the right age. She has a burning sense of injustice, having done a project on slavery, and feels instinctively that this is shared with Rames, who speaks well on the topic and the abuses. If we look ahead to the time when the episode with Rames this night is in the past, one of many of the stories that make up Connie's life and person, we will see that she maintains this sense of the need to right many wrongs, and will attempt (and, sadly, fail) to become a human rights lawyer.

She will, however, become one of the top legal secretaries – much sought after – and by the time this happens Rames will be some insignificant historical speck. It would be good to follow Connie, especially now we appear to have some substance to her. We might even give a physical description, or would that be going too far?

In the pub (can it be called a pub? – it's more of a late night drinking establishment – occasionally somebody plays jazz guitar or alt folk – I remember the original of this, eventually burnt down, we all presumed, by the owner, for insurance. It was stuck away up a back street and then up a narrow set of stairs. Actors from the local theatre often decamped there after performances.) I'm not sure it's worth going back to them in that pub right now, to be honest. Connie is more interesting than that night.

Connie

The secret to the source of Connie's jaundiced view is the tension leading up to her periods. The grand injustice of it! Everything, absolutely everything comes within her cynical, her acidly funny view of people and the world. History – a series of random events made into winningly cohesive narratives by history teachers on the side of the losers. History teachers obsess over Hitler and the Nazis: it's the parallel universe for History Teachers. Who are the history teachers in these counterfactuals? Resistance? Collaboration? Outright warriors? Sad-sack know-it-alls tut-tutting, making hopelessly false predictions? A band happens to have the same name as the Archduke of Austria-Este. What nonsense. Delete all this, it's nothing like Connie, nothing to do with her.

History – past ways of depriving people. The story of past deprivations.

More nonsense. What the tension does is give Connie's utterances a tendency towards the worst of all things, the worst possible understanding of all things. Understanding, nevertheless. Take Rames, for instance, the near-cipher. He resides in past narratives, cannot engage with the present, is a cliché of a historian, not really a historian at all and in that sense, it's the worst that can be said about him.

Or is this right in any meaningful sense? Later in life she comes round to Rames's view. Connie never loses the belief that current social injustices have identifiable historical antecedents, and may be structurally imbedded as the price of historical capitalism. Nevertheless, she begins to see (say, in her forties, early fifties?) why Rames always insisted on his students treating the past as alien to them, no matter how familiar that past might seem (*par exemple*, the downtrodden are transhistorical). No specious presentism.

Christmases

Rames continues to not celebrate Christmas (he must be well into his seventies by now if Connie is in her early fifties). He continues to not celebrate Christmas by attempting to do whatever he would do on any other day. This is now in the future, some way ahead of the writing of this, so we can only presume that the reader imagines the year 2057. Connie is looking forward to retiring from her successful career as a legal secretary, somebody who has been involved in some of the most high-profile human rights cases in the country (we can't assume the country is the same? but we can assume the law and its actors will continue to exist?). An Albanian sound designer has accidentally discovered the mechanism for teleportation, and this will become Connie's new passion in the sixties (the two-thousand and sixties) as she seeks him out. If the story were properly science fiction, she could go back to the evening after the ball and observe what happened with and to the group, herself included, and Rames. Or perhaps we would see the way in which her fascination for Sokol replaces her concern for inhumanity and make a moral out of that.

Meanwhile, in 2057, Rames is not celebrating Christmas with weary assiduity. One way to not celebrate Christmas is to wear the jumper with the glass shards (would a jumper last fifty years? Perhaps some material-enhancing spray has continued the life of the jumper beyond what we now consider feasible and he has found some kind soul to repair the frayed collar. We think we are cutting-edge, but we are past now, when we think of Connie and Rames some fifty-plus years on from the here and the now). Connie tucks in to the traditional Christmas meal (unspecified) and Rames eats ham sandwiches with Piccadilly Piccalilli (his wife refuses to not celebrate Christmas and cooks for the downtrodden a few miles down the road). While eating this he thinks of the group of five and the jumper. He puts on the jumper carefully, trying not to cut himself too much. It's been a long time since that evening of the ball, when he got drunk, and everybody felt the inevitability of Rames and Connie converging, like Gavrilo Princip and Franz Ferdinand in Sarajevo, at the start (starting?) of the first world war. 'So this is how you welcome your guest, with bombs?'

Franz Ferdinand's wife is Sophie Chotek, a maid-in-waiting, and therefore socially inappropriate for someone of Franz's standing. Perhaps if she refuses to go out that day – after all, she has to secede precedence to every bleeding archduchess in the Austro-Hungarian empire, so why not throw a strop once in a while – we can change.

Johannes Boanerges

As feared, I was made literary executor for Johannes Boanerges in the summer of 2003. My longtime friend and nowtime nemesis finally checked out of 'the great game' at the age of 104, having lived through the mass slaughter of two world wars and countless other conflicts and genocides (which, as we know, my friend did attempt to count sometime in the mid 70s, *Calling Evil to Account*). A chaos merchant himself, his papers were (are) in chaos. Nor do we have the saving grace of a systematic thinker – there is no steady progression of ideas in Boanerges, no gradual enlightenment or Damascene moments to which I can discretely attach his many outpourings; rather, a lurching from one grand idea to another throughout the twentieth century, a ready convert to the newest, shiniest, most provoking expositions, critiques, theories and dénouements the last century had to offer. And yet, and yet, at each stage he was often the most brilliant of exponents for these fads which have on occasion lingered into our present. When challenged for his inconsistency he would quote Nietzsche, his favourite creative writer: If I contradict myself, well, I contradict myself. He was happiest when promoting anti-philosophy, following in the footsteps of Lucretius, Montaigne, Nietzsche, and, on occasion, Rosset, urging us to see truth as nothing more than an army of metaphors on the march, a veil cast over the unpalatable real. And yet, and yet, we know all too well that if there is one constant in Johannes' life, it is his desire to eke out the truth, objective, eternal, universal Truth, in the face of the nay-sayers such as myself who, without relent, relish uncovering the arbitrary nature of all things (I make no bones about it). Having been made this man's executor, who would in their heart of hearts relish sifting through and making sense of eighty years worth of passionate lucidity (more if we take into account the juvenilia), foisted on the world in his many voices, the many pseudonyms Johannes insisted were the only way he could 'tell it as it is', as the Americans like to say? In his name-playing, game-playing, anti-philosophy, with its target TRUTH, we can see that Monsieur Boanerges was indeed closer in spirit to Kierkegaard, yet I have not found one mention of the troubled Dane in all the boxes, in all the published work (hence the occasional charge of plagiarism; but how much credit does Heidegger give Søren, I ask you?). Again, I ask you, under such conditions who would relish the sentence of having the duty in their remaining years to organise what cannot be organised, represent what is beyond representation, in the hope that amongst such sift the pearls of wisdom which may yet save you, me, the planet, are to be found. The real Johannes Boanerges I am convinced will ever remain a mystery – for we can know man, but not any single man (Rochefoucauld). But the biographical details are unimportant, Johannes' attempted suicides tell us nothing. We have the texts, and a few accomplished doodles, and in them, I believe we have much more than the facts of an extraordinary life, that was, if I may be permitted the hyperbole, the twentieth century encapsulated.

I have taken the opportunity of this essay title – just to remind ourselves, 'Is the human species special?' – to attempt to at least pull something together from JB's work, even if this organising fiction may have to be abandoned at a later point. 'Better to travel than to arrive', springs to mind, but you, dear reader, may object. If we do not follow the question through to a conclusion as soon as we can, or, as I would prefer to say, follow through to a compromised reconciliation that refuses to face THE TRUTH, then there will be no arrival, merely the death of another species, our own, special or otherwise (the question before us).

Johannes had much to say on what it is to be human, although not quite as directly as we might wish. I am still at the early stage of ordering and cataloguing his materials, as I have said, so really the request for this essay, which I have take upon myself in his name, comes at an inopportune moment. Another ten years of my substantial scholarly endeavour will offer firmer foundations on which to build a substantial, duly considered response, in dialogue with B's work. Nevertheless, it does provide an opportunity for me to experiment with some thematic strands on which to hang the novels, poetry, pseudo-memoirs, theatre script, libretto, emails (Boanerges – an early advocate), public and private letters, and other ephemera. JB remained open to new forms throughout his life, right to the end, what fortitude!, what stamina!, and would, I am sure, be tweeting, facebooking and blogging to his heart's content at this minute. The diversification of media, the possibilities of many-to-many communication heralded by the brilliance of the Internet, he foresaw as an untrammelled force for good (it always took him a decade to move on to the next big thing, so he had yet to lose his enthusiasm for electronic interconnectedness, as I had done early on). Our arguments around this were more general. He told me that different media facilitated a more rounded representation of TRUTH, not different truths, just as his resort to textual ventriloquism aided him in seeing the TRUTH from all angles. But we know this to simply be false. Did not the telescope and the microscope – new ways of seeing – tell us that the world was different from what we believed? These did not *add* to the sum of human knowledge, but *changed* our view forever. We keep changing our views, changing our media, changing our metaphors. There is no constant truth, no TRUTH. I would fling it in his face. After such passion he would take the calm attitude: 'You, my friend, are wrong'. I would have no choice but to leave, our arguments forever irreconcilable, but not our friendship, most importantly, for he would inevitably call me forth to dinner, prepared by his well-treated (contrary to popular opinion) companion and amanuensis, Victor(ia).

As part of this preamble I should perhaps forestall what you might see as a natural resting point. Could we not skip his life's work and turn to the back-page, glance at his last sentence, to see if our endeavours are worth the candle? At the age of 104 surely he had intimations of mortality and was intent on bequeathing to humanity what was wisest and best in a conclusive, hopefully pithy, epigram. It is true that he attempted to keep a separate set of notebooks, hidden from Victor(ia), a kind of double-accounting which only came to light after his death (did Victor[ia] know; surely s/he must have, but s/he says s/he didn't). Blind for the last fifteen years of his life, the secret books are barely legible, and written more often than not in his native Livonian language. When he died, there were fewer than twenty speakers of Livonian (one of the Uralic languages), although Boanerges always maintained that only he was alert to its subtleties and the others might as well be deceased for what they could bring to our understanding of the language. In one of the secret notebooks, not dated, but which I calculate to be the last due to the manner in which some pages are virgin, the Livonian suddenly gives way to English: 'We are no[*] dead'. [*] indicates a missing consonant. I dismiss Victor(ia)'s suggestion that it is merely a smudge, as one might expect from someone blind attempting to write in manuscript hand, and that, as s/he asserts, the outburst is none other than a sentence in the Scottish form. It is true that on occasion my friend would attempt the Scots dialect, which he had tried to connect with the Uralic language family, but there is no evidence that this found its way into his writing. No. The missing consonant is either a 't', 'We are not dead', or a 'w', 'We are now dead'. It is infuriating that we cannot ascertain with certainty his final judgement. Knowing Johannes Boanerges as I do, as nobody else does (certainly not Victor[ia], faithful though I grant s/he has been), we know it could be either interpretation: it could be that the human spirit is triumphant, 'We are not dead'; or it could be that humanity has failed, 'We are now dead'. To translate it into the theme of this question: 'We are special', 'we are not special'. Johannes, of course, would never have been so direct. That is our loss. But we must interpret, we are *homo verto*[1] – interpreting, seeking knowledge – not *homo sapiens*, 'wise man', 'knowing man', as if we are already in the promised land of being know-alls. (Victor[ia] suggests that if I must insist on inserting a consonant for the smudge, then Johan could be referring to the death [or not] of the Livonian language, or Livonians. I have told her/him that I do not think the fact s/he shared the man's bed guarantees his/her interpretation of his writing. I have no truck with biographical underpinnings. However, I must continue to be pleasant to Victor[ia] since s/he has squirreled away the private letters, memos and notes he sent to her/him. S/he will hand them over, s/he has promised, when I have finished work on the bequeathed literary materials. I trust by that time any new information coming to light will not affect what I have to finally say about the man. Victor[ia] says that I am not a scholar in any ways capable of interpreting 'marks left on a bedsheet'; an Estonian saying, s/he assures me. I hold my tongue better to profit humanity. S/he also questions my Latin. I will give her no more text time here.)

---

[1] *verto*: to turn, turn around, transform, turn up, to put to flight, rout, to turn into, transform, to flee, <u>interpret</u>, understand, upset, overthrow

Animals

And so, let us begin with his reflections on animals.

Always – on this he was insistent – he hated them. From a young age he ate as much meat as he could. We know of his religious upbringing (later rejected) and how he felt in his very marrow that man truly had been given dominion over the earth, over animals. Man's unique place in the order of things ordained by God, that man was licensed to do as he pleased. Man – more than animal, less than an angel in the Great Chain of Being – Man – Semi-Divine – chomping his way through the animal kingdom. This, Johannes maintained, God had decreed. I can only see this as a species of sarcastic pride – Socratic pride, daring by his actions to force God or the animals to retort. Even his brief and only spell in India, there as a journalist reporting on the Beatles, did nothing to convince him of the spiritual merit of vegetarianism. But I concede Victor(ia) may be right at least on this point. How are we to read him and his behaviour in relation to animals and the name that signifies their very death and our great superiority, 'meat'? Of the many references to animals in his writing, we here relate just two items.

The first item, as is well known, is his pig-husbandry. He kept pigs and never ate the ones he reared. Sure, he would taunt them with the waft of bacon emerging from his kitchen, and brazenly eat his beloved BEST[1] in front of them, and this may seem to some of us cruel. But for Johannes this was man communing with animal, offering the chance for the most intelligent of animals to speak, to indicate where man's arrogance was unwarranted. At the end of each session he would rise from his favoured wicker chair (think van Gogh) and rising say 'The pig speaketh not'. He would turn to walk away, then suddenly turn back to see if they were talking about him, to see if they had conversation, culture, ideas. But nothing. He would give them the best of his thought. But nothing. 'The pig speaketh not'. There is a yearning in his pig diaries (covers made out of pig skin! written in the finest of artist's brushes derived from pig bristles!) to discover elements of the human, to give the animal world the chance to speak back, to enter into dialogue, to demonstrate in fact (in the language of this essay) that humans are *not* special. But

[1]   BEST = 'bacon, egg, sausage, tomato'

without language, culture, abstract thought, the will to power, the ability to hold sway over the universe and bend it to its needs, the animal kingdom as exemplified by Boanerges' beloved pigs proved beyond doubt that humankind is special (JB began to adopt 'humankind' in place of 'mankind' at the start of the 1980s, after the American controversy around his probable bigamous past, as well as related accusations of systemic misogyny; see below). And if there is no God, or Gods, and no angels, reasoned Boanerges, a position he came to like many others after knowledge of the nature of the Shoah crept up on an unbelieving world after 1945 – is this what it is to be human? is this what humans can do? no other animal has achieved this – then there truly is nothing like the human. There followed his period of despair, exacerbated by a continued attraction to the tenets of Sartre and his crew, but all the time in the background of his mind, tempering his despair, his sneer that 'this is what makes us special – genocide' – tempering this was the belief that if there is the capacity for infinite evil there is the capacity for infinite good. 'What if', he started to muse, 'what if our difference from the animals is our ability to do infinite good, our ability to progress, despite these setbacks, to *know* what good is and to reconfigure social, political, cultural and economic orders to achieve this?' It was the Enlightenment project viewed as a discontinuous but nevertheless upward trajectory. As we can observe at this distance, such questioning was the background to that major unfinished opus, *What if?* Although he had started to look elsewhere by the end of the 1980s, turning away from all Enlightenment heritage in favour of a brief flirtation with Gaia, he formally declared the 'What if?' project 'dead and buried' in July 1994 with the Rwandan genocide of almost a million people, while the world watched and did nothing. Nothing! I know that Victor(ia), who had just come into his life in 1991, attempted to apply some racist excuse, blaming it on a backwards Africa, to jolly him out of this renewed slough of despond and fourth suicide attempt. And it is true that for a while even the events in Rwanda did not quite end his belief in a discontinuous but positive outcome to the project of Enlightenment; he held his judgement in abeyance. But then came Srebenica the following year and the slaughter of 8,000. That was it. The arguments over a certain moral equivalence between perpetrators and victims simply reminded him of the ongoing arguments over the Armenian genocide of a million plus people. Holocaust denial – Armenia, (Nazi) Germany, Rwanda,

Srebenica – the pattern repeated. Nothing could bring him back to the philosophical/anti-philosophical tradition after that. He would have to look elsewhere. At the end of some notes on these holocausts he scrawls, in English, 'exterminate the brutes', in mock recognition of his own human status and complicity by species association, and in echo of Conrad's death-knell for Enlightenment, with Kurtz maddened at the end of Enlightenment projections.

The second item relating to animals is the image (sound) of snow monkeys in winter. David Attenborough can be heard describing the look on their faces as they wait for the winter ice to melt. They are *waiting*, not in an intense predatory way, as a creature attends upon its prey, but just sitting around *waiting*. The word that Attenborough uses to describe the look on their faces is *boredom*. Along with ideas about 'nothingness', what Boanerges had taken from Existentialism into other areas of thought was a notion that 'boredom' was the essence of the human. An animal could not be bored in its animal existence Boanerges once wrote. And here they were – nothing to do with their ability to pass on knowledge of potato-peeling, an earlier Attenborough film that had impressed Boanerges and many had taken as evidence that culture – the transmission of knowledge from one generation to the next – existed in monkey world – here were *bored monkeys*. His pigs had never been bored in their animal existence. But these monkeys lived a life of Beckettian *ennui*, they couldn't go on, but they had to go on (living, I mean). These monkeys knew about the nothingness at the heart of human existence, the nothingness that only humans know.

As an aside I should say that the changing attitude towards what did and what did not constitute the animal and the human did not affect Johannes' meat-eating in the slightest. He may have shifted from a position of human arrogance to one of appreciation for the larger mammals and primates, but all that happened was his justification (when I pushed him) shifted: to eat an animal is to respect it, to take it into your body is to merge with the animal. Did this mean that we were no more than animals? 'We are part animal' he declared, but didn't elaborate. A child of seven could have told me this. He seemed to have gone backward in his thinking. And I maintain that the fact he continued to eat meat until his final successful suicide attempt showed a continuing hatred of animals. I'm not taking the moral high-ground here, more of a mid-table plateau, since I eat fish.

47

Nothingness

One of the themes that undoubtedly will make it through to the final cut is Boanerges' meditations on nothingness. Here, I think, he rivals Sartre, although the late arrival of *The Empty Bins* in 1963, twenty years after the appearance of J-P's magnum opus, has led to inevitable accusations of 'derivative'. Yet Johannes reinscribes Heidegger's 'time' into Sartre's account of being by considering the nothingness in the consciousness of the newborn babe. Sartre has nothing to say of child cognition and neo-natal consciousness. Does the newborn babe have what we would recognise as 'consciousness'? Is the newborn babe fully human? (Johannes did not think it his place to tackle the issue of foetus consciousness, so I leave it to one side, though some contradictory evidence is extant). This was the question JB posed, likening our 'early time' and our 'late time' (senility) as eras of consciousnesslessness (an inelegant term which did not help Boagernes' cause; yet there is a current move to instate Thomas Hardy's 'existlessness' as viable – are you kidding me?). 'What of the spastic, deaf and dumb three year-old?', Boanerges continues, in the revised edition (later removed when such categories became unacceptable). 'They are without language, thought, communication, consciousness – for Sartre they are not human'. But were they human for JB? In truth, he shilly-shallies. 'It depends', he begins in response to his own question, 'upon what you mean by "human"'. This is the master in his worst rhetorical phase. What redeems the book are his lyrical descriptions of moments of nothingness, when the despair of loneness overtakes him and he contemplates suicide, the only serious question, according to Camus, that philosophy needs to concern itself with. 'Why not kill your *self*?' Most people don't, Camus says, not out of deep thought on the subject, but out of a kind of 'going on', perhaps rather in the manner of the snow monkeys.

In one passage he places the gun on the table and stares at it until it becomes an emblem of existence: nothing happens unless he acts; who is he to act?; he could shoot the next person to come into the room if he chooses (this would have been his second or third wife, most likely, although he doesn't mention the fact), or, better to profit humanity, he could shoot himself. For what good is he to the world? Will the world be any the worse for his extinction? He thinks not. He has done nothing but try to be clever and write down his thoughts, many of them negative, many of them nihilistic. Will the world be better for his going? Most likely, for he will not be able to pour more despair to add to the sum of despair that already exists. But, he goes on, this is only what *he* is thinking. It is his feelings that overwhelm, that the world would be better without the human race, and that if he has no right to kill others, he at least can set his own lands in order, set an example, accompanied by a perfectly rational, coolly argued suicide note. He mentions Sartre, that it is only through human consciousness that the world comes into existence: neither element pre-exists the other, it is a mutual event, the existence of the world and the existence of the human consciousness. (Sartre just says 'consciousness', for it is presumed animals do not have consciousness). As my good friend Johannes Boagernes caresses the pearl butt with the tips of his fingers, bringing death and nothingness to his own consciousness through the fine wires in his hands, arms, neck, cerebrum, he understands it integrally as an ethical consciousness, something Sartre failed to do. He understands that it is only with human consciousness that evil is brought into the world. If we eliminate human consciousness, we eliminate evil at one stroke. Everything becomes as it was, everything returns to *the thing in itself, not* the thing perceived, for there is no longer human consciousness to bring things into existence. At once Johannes understands the beauty of the nihil. There is something about the beauty of the gun, its potential for death, its potential to rebalance the universe in favour of the universe if the gun is turned against the human self, that is inspirational. Johannes feels an uplift in his heart. At last! One act that can mean something, that can make the world a better place. He sits down to write the note before killing himself, in order to explain that he is 'emptying bins', and that this is all any of us can reasonably do.

As he starts to write the note he thinks of 1 Corinthians 13 and the difference in interpretation between the King James Version of *agape* – 'charity' – and other versions – invariably 'love', because he wants to write that this is 'a final, true act of love' or, more simply, 'an act of charity': 'Though I speak with the tongues of men and of angels, and have not love/charity, I am become *as* sounding brass, or a tinkling cymbal'; 'Love/Charity suffereth long, *and* is kind'; 'And now abideth faith, hope, charity/love, these three; but the greatest of these *is* charity/love'. In what he would have recognised as his own unoriginality, he wanted to sign off with some allusion to this well-worn passage.

But if the word were interpreted as 'love' then it were a lie, the lie all writers and philosophers and artists had perpetuated. He would be kidding himself. Hadn't he always kidded himself that the human race was better than it truly was? 'Love' was an invention covering a multitude of sins, many of which he knew he had committed. But if the less likely, the less accepted interpretation were accepted, if KJV was right, he could live with it, he could live with the idea that charity trumped all, because here was true selflessness, here was something a man could commit to, here was not nothing ('love' he knew was chimeric). A commitment to charity was a leap of faith that he believed himself to be capable of, it was an engagement with the world on positive terms. It was something he could do. And the longer the suicide note became, detailing these quibbles of interpretation, expounding on the nature of 'charity' as the antithesis to 'nothingness', the more the possibility of his suicide receded into the distance. For now, Johannes was to live on, although, famously, he refused to take up charitable causes, arguing that they helped nobody but the servants of capitalism. It is here, I think, we might draw on his earlier political writings.

Illustrations of Political Folly

Originally designed in the format of a comic book to appeal to adults and children alike, Boanerges reverted to pure prose when he had finally to admit to himself that draughtsmanship was one skill he would never master. In the thirties, having moved back to London after the heady Paris salons of the twenties (he was a favourite of Gertrude Stein) he was inevitably taken hold of by the necessity to be political (his hatred of Freud remained throughout his life, so only one of these gods were his to worship). The simple tales were designed to bring Marx to the masses, to show why capitalism was a failure, although he had the intelligence never to subscribe to communism *tout court*. Again, some of his most lyrical passages deal with the nothingness that haunts the human. Here it was in the alienation that machinery had created in man's condition, it was the alienation that capitalism had induced. He was able to simply and effectively describe the mind-numbing monotony of industrial capitalism, how the workers had nothing but their labour and their hands.

He pitched the reader headlong into the horrors of the Victorian factory system, paraphrasing Engels and Dickens. Unfortunately, he was also swayed by another of those thirties idols in the face of capitalism's crisis – the need for a strong man at the helm. And indeed, it is his most popular tale which best reveals his thinking at this time.

In the story of 'Captain Peter' we have an elemental town in which Mr Symes's cotton mill dominates the Lancashire landscape. Symes is not a bad Master, and the Men's wages are certainly sufficient to keep them reasonably well-fed. He is concerned for their welfare, and will sub a man (up to a point) when laid off sick. The cynics say that he ploughs back into his workforce just enough of his profits to ensure that future generations of workers can be reproduced and committed to his business. The workers do not see this, however, blind as they are to the true conditions of their existence, so there is no immediate reason for the workers to rebel against their lot, especially when they compare their own conditions with those conditions across the Pennines (a hill formation that separates the county of Lancashire from that of Yorkshire). But then, as JB writes it (under the pseudonym of 'The Rattener') two more mills are established on the edges of the same town, in direct competition. The following years are unsettled: sometimes the owners collude in keeping down the wages; at others they engage in skullduggery and commercial espionage. Both of these, 'The Rattener' makes clear, are accepted as modes of capitalism, in the early days, 'monopoly capitalism' and just 'capitalism'. The government is brought in and is placed in the role of policeman, judge, jury, enforcer. However capitalism decides to promote itself, the nation state agrees to underwrite its follies.

Where 'Captain Peter' differs from this usual Marxist analysis is in its criticism of the way liberal democracy – a political system – is enmeshed with capitalism – an economic system. Fed up with their lot under the vicissitudes of the three captains of capitalism, the listening government gives all the men the vote (women are not mentioned in this text). The first system of democracy they attempt awards votes to the party with the largest majority. In the first election the winning party has 51%, the losing party 49%. Although the two parties have diametrically opposed manifestoes, the supporters of the losing party must submit to the dictates of the winners. This is tyranny of the majority, and comes to be reviled by all, since at some point everyone suffers the life of a loser. The system then moves to alternative voting. The problem with this, as they soon come to see, is that political arrangements reflect nobody's preferred outcome. The third democratic system they try is proportional representation, but by this time there are no fewer than twelve parties, and the sight of twelve largely contradictory ideologies attempting to agree on a strategy as the Second World War looms is not edifying. The tale is so convincing, so plausible in its display of the failure of democracy that the reader is desperate for the solution. Enter 'Captain Peter'. He has scaled K2, discovered the largest cave system in the world in Papua New Guinea, and helped stave off the encroachments of America into a number of Latin American countries. It is clear that only a man of his personal charisma and capacity can save the day and make things work. Taking his cue from the anarcho-syndicalists, and putting all governance in the hands of the workers, Captain Peter will ensure that capitalism is overthrown and each worker gets his due rewards. When the system is stable, Captain Peter will melt back into the rank and file. Only when we are truly equal as workers, only when we have over-thrown the dehumanising effects of capitalism, will we return to our fully organic nature and system.

At this point in his career, Johannes couldn't have been clearer about human nature. Capitalism obscured what we could be as humans because at base it is exploitative – only by somebody losing can somebody win. Get the economic system right, and you get 'the human'. Get the economic system wrong and you get the 'less than human'. If consciousness brought evil into the world, as he later argued (see above), capitalism brought the human as subhuman into being. Johannes was adamant: capitalism *cannot* be ameliorated. Throughout that part of globalisation that Mr Boanerges saw in the latter part of the twentieth century he argued that he was essentially correct, that the cheap goods of the developed world were at the expense of Bangladeshi children. As soon as there was nowhere in the world that agreed to work for peanuts, capitalism would collapse. Although Boanerges managed to keep up his left-wing rhetoric throughout the rest of his life, his critics always had at hand his failure to see how Captain Peter was none other than Uncle Joe Stalin to come. How much did he truly subscribe to marxian economics, and how much of it was an adopted pose? I believe he truly thought that it was in humankind's hands to make itself human through correct application of socialist theory, and he believed that you could not 'add on' an economic system to 'the human'. Bad systems made for a subhuman species. Only by creating and sustaining a system that allows every single individual in the world to participate in beneficence can humans truly be called 'human'; only then can we say that as a species we have become 'human'. Otherwise the 'human' will have to remain an idea, thwarted by the numerous exploitations the world's inadequate politico-economic systems enforce under the managerial hymn of 'the least worst'.

Some of this thinking found its way into another book he planned, first as a novel, then as a political tract, finally as a narrative poem, provisionally entitled *Why Not?* He said we needed the world to stop for a week (other than emergency services) so that we could reflect on the best way forward. 'Why not?' becomes the refrain in all these versions. He was working toward the yoking of the demise of capitalism with the revivification of Gaia, but the notes are too tentative to be included here. I may develop them elsewhere, perhaps integrated with our duty to bear witness, both to our atrocious behaviour and to our need to attend more fully to our place in the organic realm. It may be that 'nature' is as much the 'face of the other' as our fellow humans, and that we need to embrace the asymmetric I-thou of this relationship. But that would be *me* talking, not my friend Johannes, and me talking in a good mood at that, as you no doubt surmise.

Conclusion

I have not spoken much about Johannes Boargenes' life, although I have hinted at its extraordinary nature. What does it benefit us to know that he may not have been born in Finland, but rather in Smyrna, and removed to Scandinavia some time around 1905? It might make him seem more cosmopolitan, but what else? And what of the now-established fact that, as was rumoured during his first American lecture tour in 1966, he had left behind in Italy in 1929 a Jewish wife and two children. They survived by making their way Eastwards – Malaysia, Indonesia, the Philippines. True, the evidence shows he sent numerous remittances to them, even when he married and remarried (without ever having divorced Rebeccah), but he never once openly acknowledged their existence. Was the protection of Victor(ia), who knew them, some kind of penitence, some kind of atonement? But again, what have these biographical details to do with the man's ideas? Would you reject the cure for cancer because it came from a man who kept slaves?

I conclude (provisionally, of course – this is a work-in-progress) with two unrelated items, which, if there is such a thing as 'the human' in the sense of 'special', may yet be connected at some deep level. (If it were left to me I would leave you with another saying from Rochefoucauld: 'No man is wise enough to know all the evil he does', but this is not about me, and what do I know?)

When Johannes fled the October Revolution with some Romanov hangers-on (his aristocratic tendencies were still intact then), he took with him an unfired clay head, originally from Aï Khanum in Afghanistan, and over 2000 years old. The face is serene, eyes blind or just closed, the mouth relaxed, certainly not smiling, but perhaps with a laconic understatement hovering at the lips. This, Victor(ia) assures me, was amongst the effects he bequeathed her/him, although s/he will not let me view it (I have only a photograph). Victor(ia) also tells me that this relic was what Joho (his/her name for Johannes) aspired to; this was what he wanted his death mask to look like. I saw an exhibition by the Spanish sculptor Jaume Plensa (2011, Yorkshire Sculpture Park), which included large alabaster heads. We were not allowed to touch these delicacies, despite their size, as if the sculptor had imbued them with a newly-minted double millennia of fragility. They had the same look, across twenty centuries, the same look, I swear.

But is it boredom on the old face and the new ones, rather than a know-ledgeable serenity? What would Johannes have said? That they are not human? The human cannot be here? Nearly human? Not human, not yet, not yet? I doubt it. He would have mischievously, viciously even, dependent upon his mood, have referred us to the phrase he most dreaded, the phrase his first son greeted him with every morning:

'I'm bored. What are we going to do today?'

Ham

Kevin the most famous moved into caves with his Uncle and the others. The Emperor's men would find them later, there was no doubt, so they moved deep into the system to the penultimate space in order to defer the inevitability of their joint fate. The last cave was for utter despair only, so they let it alone.

Valerie was a short stocky woman with jet-black hair dyed using simples which she kept secret. Her daughter was on the outside and Valerie began to tell the assembly of her daughter's love for hamsters until Kevin's Uncle, a tall gangly man with beady eyes, said they had more pressing things, 'like avoiding death by a thousand cuts', an evasion which they knew could not be theirs. They turned to Kevin the most famous and asked him what to do, giving all rights over their lives to him. Instead of thinking about them as a group and the responsibility he had now acquired, not entirely unwelcome to him it has to be said, Kevin pondered his own survival. There was something about the situation that demanded he bear witness, that demanded he live to tell all inhabitants of the City State, even if it meant all of them excepting the most famous person perished.

'I need time to think'.

Most of them respected Kevin's request for a mental clearing. Those who didn't said that there wasn't time, something had to be done immediately about food, water, wine and human waste.

'We can defend the cave without any problems because of the narrow entrance and its incline – they will not attack until a week has gone and they can be sure we are weak. We have the inner light from our diverse technologies, so that's no problem'. They were all calmed by this. Only Kevin remained agitated. As time went by some of the group attempted to win his favour, as if this would improve their chances of survival, for the chance of survival appeared to rest with Kevin. There was a human form of sorts towards the back of the cave who was more intelligent than Kevin, yet owing to its ill-designed shape did not attract the seekers of wisdom. If they asked it it would tell them how some of them could escape as a group, yet Kevin worried that this would not guarantee his own survival and he could not be sure that the creature would not gain in self-confidence over the coming days as looks became less important and the ability to reason became paramount.

'It is inevitable we will die, and it is inevitable we will need to eat each other'. Others had already come to the same conclusion. 'Better we face this sooner'. He looked at the creature at the back of the cave and the others looked back at it as well. The seeds were sown for the first meal and the removal of the most intelligent of them all, the creature who could save some of them but could not guarantee a named individual's survival.

Valerie's Daughter

She came down in the night to find the hamster upside down biting the wire that formed the cage ceiling. Valerie's daughter was desperate; the veil over existence had been drawn back and here was the horror of the caged hamster, doomed for eternity to a futile biting existence. Taking the little fellahin out she did her best to comfort it, and for a while it was happy to play on the table, running to an edge and stopping, turning back on itself to the opposite edge and repeating the manoeuvre. Valerie's daughter – the group could not remember the daughter's name – had given the hamster 'many loves', and the hamster had absorbed all. It stopped now, lost interest in itself, and much to her dismay wanted to go back in the cage. Cupping it with many loves she placed it back in the cage and replaced the wire top. The hamster immediately took to hanging by its two front feet from the wire top, swinging across the vast expanse of construction (as it appeared to the fellahin's mind) like an ape on jungle vines.

Some of the group wandered away from Valerie's story. The daughter wasn't there in the cave with them, she was just in Valerie's head, so what was the point? The ones who stayed to listen to the end of the story did so out of nostalgia for the world they had been forced to leave behind. 'Yes' said Kevin, spying an opportunity, 'yes. I can go and speak for us all. Get them to let us back in. Shall I go and speak for us all? It is our best hope. I am, after all, famous for my ability to speak for groups'. Everyone pondered without speaking.

Inside Kevin

Inside Kevin were a number of schemes for getting himself out alive. The best was to speak on their behalf in a famous manner, which would be self-confirming, and not to worry too much if he had to sell them down the river in doing so. The advantage of them all dying except him was that they would not live to accuse or contradict him. He had taught rhetoric to the Emperor's sons and knew that they remained fond of him. His and the others' disagreement with his majesty could be resolved to the latter's satisfaction at the group's expense, it seemed to Kevin, while at the same time the Emperor's continuing love for Kevin, and the love for him of the Emperor's sons, would ensure this. The many loves of the Emperor and his offspring would ensure this. Kevin smiled, projecting this idea outwards.

Outside Kevin

The Uncle knew his nephew better than anyone else there (about thirty of them, a veritable tribe) and had always come off worst against the nephew's silvery tongue. Against this he pitted Valerie's daughter's hamster's cage, forcing analogies. Kevin was shaken. Seizing the moment, the Uncle moved on to a scenario where the supporters of the Emperor and his finery would force their way into the cave, up the narrow incline, happy to lose people on the way because of what was at stake, namely, the Emperor and all he stood for in a City State. Kevin changed tack.

'It doesn't have to be me!'

'I'm the tallest', said his Uncle, who wasn't quite, 'so I should go. Kevin will sell you down the river. I never would'.

'It is fine for somebody else to go', said Kevin, 'but we need the person to speak well for us. Being tall does not vouchsafe good talking. We need someone experienced in the art of rhetoric'.

'We are morally right', said Alexandra, a tall thin woman not unlike a female version of Kevin's Uncle and a tad higher, 'so there is no need to depend upon your fancy arguments, Kevin. If the Emperor is moral he will understand and release us because that's the right thing to do. Besides, which of us wants to live in an unjust Kingdom? If the Emperor doesn't understand that it's right to let us go on living in the city then we should die, all of us, together, life will not be worth living. I would come back and die with you'. She cracks knuckles to emphasise her main points, which none of the others can do.

'Yes, you're right, Alexandra'.

Another said that it would be safest to kill themselves there and then rather than be taken alive. Since they had spent some time in the cave and the situation was deteriorating with stuffiness, smells and hunger, there was a general acceptance of this, mainly because it was more in keeping with their moral compass and sense of honour.

'He is right. Let's kill ourselves honourably'.

After some thought Kevin agreed this was a good idea. They could draw straws or some other mechanism to decide on the order of the deaths. The difficulty was the last two standing, probably Kevin and his Uncle, who had a mutual distrust. The group could see the value in this since the relatives were sure to kill each other and there would be honour.

Inside Kevin

Inside Kevin were the thoughts of opportunity. There was something to be said for a mechanism whereby all of the group bar him and his Uncle were removed since his chances of survival would be significantly increased. Inside Kevin was the belief that he could persuade the Emperor to any significant end he chose, including the sparing of his life.

The thought was there, too, that with the others out the way he could convince his Uncle that there was only one of them who could relate to everybody outside the cave system the terrible ordeal the group had faced, and the necessity to die with honour. They would trust someone already well-known like himself, less so a mere relative of the famous person.

Two Hamsters

Valerie related the time before the one hamster to those who wanted to listen to stories from the old world. The one that had survived into the first story was called Tracey. In the time before the one hamster, the period of 'Two Hamsters', the daughter put Tracey and Sharon in the same cage because she had been told this breed of hamster was sociable and she looked forward to this era of harmonious side-by-sides. She had called them Tracey and Sharon because the names were exotic and foreign and because she was an Anglophile. It was not long before her dream was undone, when the frantic squeals of Tracey communicated to the world that Sharon was scratching Tracey's belly raw. This continued for a few days, the daughter hoping that it was initial teething problems, until she had to separate them, seeing that Tracey was passive under Sharon's aggression. Understandably, Tracey thrived in her solitary existence, the daughter often taking it out and putting it on tables where it would rush to the edge past all the playful tiny obstacles strategically placed. Sharon however took a turn for the worse, even though she had been the more robust when in the cage violently bullying Tracey, and became seriously enervated. The daughter half-heartedly tried to heat it up, but the magnified squeals of Tracey haunting the daughter's waking dreams meant that she was not sorry to watch Sharon die, by which time Tracey's stomach had healed and the fur returned. The daughter fashioned an ermine outfit from the dwarf stoat she also kept and crowned Tracey 'Her Most Mighty Sweet Tracey Empress' for her greatness and passive temperament. 'My Sweet Empress' and 'My Sweet Tracey' were her favourite epithets. Valerie wanted to emphasise the 'sweet' nature of the hamster to her audience, emerging as she had done from the horrors inflicted by Sharon.

Although the story of the 'Two Hamsters' entertained some of the tribe, the others were not to be deflected from the real poignancy of their predicament. It was now fourteen days into the retreat and the forging of a bunker mentality. They had heard noises and seen some flickering shapes towards the bottom of the narrow incline and had been afraid. Why didn't their pursuers try smoking them out, like animals in underground dens? Did they want them to come out instead and be captured alive of their own free will? When Kevin heard these musings he saw an opportunity to press once again for his role as the group's ambassador. 'They would like to treat with us', he said. 'They realise the justness of our plight, as Alexandra has urged'. Alexandra disputed Kevin's taking in hand of her ideas. The others wanted only to hear Kevin, who once more was showing leadership qualities, qualities which held the group together for another three weeks, by which time they were eating their shoes and belts.

'It is time to die', said Alexandra.

'What would Tracey do?', some asked.

The creature at the back spoke for the first time, but it was difficult to understand it because the fat in their ears was long gone. In essence they were lip-reading, and following its pointing paw and nails in the direction of Kevin the famous. The creature acknowledged Kevin's superior rhetorical powers, and was sure that Kevin would be able to fashion a suitable and powerful argument to the Emperor that might or might not be persuasive, not that it was doubting Kevin's rhetorical ability. What it doubted was the Emperor's mind, which none of them had been inside, not even Kevin. It took an hour for the creature to make this much known through positive signs and contra-moues.

The Uncle was the closest to death of all of them and asked 'What would Tracey do, what would the Sweet Empress do?' He insisted on standing, for if he were going to die it would be standing. Alexandra, who was the only person who could stand shoulder-to-shoulder with him, whispered into a fatless ear that Tracey would do the right thing. The Uncle sat back down muttering 'the right thing' and Kevin picked up on this. He seemed to have fared better than all of them, seemed not to have hunger or disease or mental illness, seemed to glow when he spoke in the light of their technologies, seemed not to smell of faeces.

'I can do the right thing for us all. I have seen inside the Emperor's mind. It is arbitrary, but can be persuaded to do the right thing if a man is allowed to speak the right things to him. Only I know this, for I have partly been responsible for tutoring his mind, his mind is partly my education. Do you understand? I know it is hard to understand with fatless ears and empty stomachs. I am the only one who has ever been close enough to step inside the Emperor's very head'.

It was very difficult to decide between the Mighty Sweet Empress Tracey, Kevin, and the creature at the back of the cave. Valerie began to speak of a later time when Tracey had fought off the attentions of a large, mean-spirited ginger cat. The cat had been nearly blind and Tracey had used this to her advantage, tricking the cat almost into bringing Tracey food instead of eating her. The small group which had followed all of Valerie's stories keenly understood that they were as good as inside Valerie. Kevin saw the thirty-or-so-people splinter before him and made one last attempt to bring them back into one people. 'I will see the Emperor. We, you, I have nothing to lose and everything to gain'. The creature tempted the group with honour and said that it was now time to contemplate what they could not contemplate before – the last cave. It was down a steep incline and then through a vertical drop and so there was no way back. Alexandra wondered what the advantage would be. 'Wouldn't it take longer to die?', she cracked, 'wouldn't it? wouldn't it? Let's kill ourselves now'. The Uncle said it was the right thing to kill themselves now. They unsheathed tiny double-edged daggers in preparation.

Inside Kevin Inside the Emperor

Some of the rooms inside the Emperor's head were full of clutter, some were harems, some were granaries, and some were jumbled arguments. 'It is not unlike a complicated system of caves' inside Kevin opined in the cave of empathy to the Emperor's representative there. Whelmed by sorrow inside Kevin longed to move into future caves and projected himself into a cave devoted to the objects the Emperor had acquired. Inside Kevin found himself there and became despondent as he gazed long and hard from inside to the outside Kevin inside the Emperor's cave of acquisitions. He tried deviously to move this Kevin into the cave where he had been whelmed by sorrow. Why wasn't he there? The Emperor's representative said it stood to reason objects were not allowed in that cave. How then was inside Kevin to make the most of being inside the Emperor?

61

Goodbye

Kevin the famous said farewell to the thirty-or-so-people, not daring to glance back as they prepared to thrust the tiny daggers into their hearts through the gaps in their rib cages. There were no noises behind him as he moved onwards, no groans of death and honour to egg him on, these would have to be invented in his head to offer the Emperor, the story of his people that would save his life, that he would recount until his own natural death, with fantastical descriptions of the caves' crystalline sheens. The glory of his people who had died for what they believed. He would ask the Emperor that the cave system be sealed off to prevent any State citizens intruding on the cave spirits. Kevin knew that this would ensure only his version would prevail.

Hello

The final cave has been previously stocked by the creature with enough food for a year, particularly cured meats, and the creature leads those left behind to it. They realise the despair of the cave and see now why the creature has the form that it does for it has known all along, for they cannot die now, for there is nothing they can have believed in. They eat the finest pickles knowing they should have died in the penultimate cave. They linger here, admiring and resenting the creature who will lead them out in a year through the elaborate honeycombs through to the other side of the mountain, the side which struggles with the sun.

Whim

We found the meter man humourless and locked him in the cellar. At first he didn't seem to realise because he was reading the gas and electric and then he did realise when he couldn't get out and started banging on the door, though not as much as we thought he might. Our suspicions about his humourlessness were confirmed because he thought the whole thing might be a joke, so we had to explain we'd done it on a whim, which was different. This calmed him down, somewhat, or made him think. After a while he started banging again and shouting, perhaps annoyed that we were splitting hairs over whether it was a joke or a whim.

We went out of the house for a bit because we couldn't stand the noise and re-entered quietly a couple of hours later. The meter man was silent. Hopefully he had accepted his fate. The cat started fussing for its tea and we realised the mistake we'd made – the catfood was at the top of the cellar, 'the cellar head', so we couldn't get it without opening the door and giving the meter man a chance to escape. We could try to ascertain if he was down the bottom of the cellar, quickly open the door, snatch the food, close and lock, but that seemed risky. It was obvious we hadn't thought the locking up of the meter man through, and we came close at that point – closer than we have ever been before or since – close to dreary domestic wrangling. What was happening to us? We were changing, 'transforming'. We just couldn't seem to reconcile ourselves to the situation. But after a few days, we did (reconcile ourselves), buying in more catfood for instance, rather than wishing and hoping to get at the cellarhead catfood which was now out of bounds.

During those few days a number of logical problems cropped up which may have occurred to you as you've been reading. We had no wish to cause the meter man unnecessary distress through lack of food and water. Luckily there is a coal-chute into the cellar from outside. It has bars at the bottom of the chute to stop burglars breaking and entering, and now, as we realised, could just as easily function to stop people getting out. Through the gaps in the bars we could throw down food and drink. As to pissing and shitting, he'd just have to live in his own filth, that was just the way it was, and he could fulfil his sexual needs by masturbating, if he was so inclined, which we suspected he was. If he got bored he could read the meters. The other thing was that the cellar's at ground level, and there's a small dirty window which he could smash. We don't know what happened, but it didn't seem to occur to him to smash it and shout. Certainly it would be difficult to break because there were bars in front of the glass, yet not impossible. In order that nobody could see or hear him through the small barred glass window, we blocked off the front entrance to our house and asked people to come round to the back of the house, which is not uncommon in this part of Yorkshire for some unfathomable reason. The gas and electric rang us to see if we'd been visited, which spooked us because then it occurred to us he might have a phone. That was something else we hadn't thought of. 'Why don't you phone him?', we double-bluffed. 'We've tried', they said, 'but his phone's switched off'. So he didn't have it on him, otherwise he could've just phoned, couldn't he? They agreed. It seemed a rather pointless conversation after that.

During those few days, even though we nearly changed at the point we came close to dreary domestic wrangling, we didn't actually change very much at all, and our mutual love continued unabated. We retained an air of smugness, which we had always enjoyed to be honest, and found that very self-conceitedness to be enhanced since we knew full well that the current poor economic climate and deteriorating environmental conditions outside had barely touched us. Our lives were continuing pretty much as before, and we really were enjoying having the meter man in the cellar, and thought it a good antidote to the recent (past two or three years) negative press regarding keeping people in cellars.

We're talking about spring, moving into summer here, just in case you need to get your chronological bearings, and typically we were getting April showers in June. What's happening to the weather? everybody was asking at that time, I remember. It was one night about two weeks into our escapade

64

when a funny thing happened. We were settled in bed waiting to enter the Land of Nod when it started raining. Our bed is in the attic conversion, so rain on the roof is quite noticeable. We got up to look out the window at the rain, but there was no rain. There was the sound of rain, *but there was no rain!* This spooked us, really spooked us, so we removed the access panel to the header tank, which was placed (is placed, in fact, it's still there) above the headboard. With the panel gone the noise got louder. It was too late to do anything about it that night. We could look into it again the next morning, perhaps ask the meter man in the cellar if he had any ideas about what the cause of the noise of the rain was *when we couldn't see any rain!* We went to sleep wondering if there were such a thing as invisible rain, a rather fantastic idea, which kept us amused and proved to be our passport to entering the Land of Nod. Part of us, we were sure, hoped that the noise would simply disappear by morning. Was this too much to ask? If it hadn't gone by the morning, we might ask the meter man in the cellar if he had any ideas (we kept saying this to ourselves about asking the meter man in the cellar if he had any ideas, for reassurance, replacing our usual nighttime repetitions. In a strange way that night we came to rely on the meter man in the cellar).

The next day the noise was still there. We shouted down to the meter man if he had any ideas, which was partly our way of checking to see that he was still all right. He did shout back, which was good, but with unrelated responses, which was unhelpful. Having no luck there, we ran back up to the top of the house, removed the access panel again, and heard the noise louder than ever, sounding something like halfway between rain on the roof (it still wasn't raining) and something like a huge insect scraping away behind the insulation boards. It really was a puzzle. We discovered that banging on the boards stopped the noise for a short time, only for it to start up again, as if it had politely waited to see if our banging meant something and we were going to continue. Rather like the meter man in the cellar though, we couldn't just stay there banging forever, it was something we had to accept. Well, sort of. We phoned John and he came round to have a look. The most obvious solution, which he himself suggested, was that there was a wasp's nest behind the insulation boards. He went away after a cup of coffee and we phoned a pest control company.

Carl hated Birmingham and the South. The noise, he said, was a wasp's nest, in phase two of development, and he showed us a couple of the wasp babies. He said we were lucky it wasn't a bee's nest because they were now protected by law and couldn't be killed, only moved. 'What would we do then, if it was a bee's nest?', we asked, because it was not possible to get into the space behind the boards where the nest was. We were worried for some reason, even though it was a wasp's nest. 'Nothing. Sleep where you can't hear it. They'd be gone by October. They wouldn't hurt you'. The wasp's nest had to be killed off. The noise of rain was wasps chewing wood and insulation and making glue for the nest. Imagine! Just a few inches away from your head as you sleep! 'You can get up to ten thousand wasps in a nest', he said. As soon as he said that we just wanted him to get the thing over and done with. He chatted a bit longer, said that people were looking for aliens in outer space when really wasps were aliens, and he said he thought there might be a problem with our drains (that was probably the piss and shit from the gas and electric meter man – we thought we'd masked the smell!), and Carl got changed into his space-suit, and exploded something that killed off the nest. Hurrah!

II

He thought he could become the other gasman, the other one, now that all his neurons and protoplasm and cell walls were in place, as described in the biology primer left for him on top of the meter. The overwhelming problem was the arrangement of internal organs. These had been assembled carelessly, as if their minds were elsewhere. Still, now that he was resigned to his fate, he could concentrate on this. 'I miss making my own meat'. These words interfered whenever he wanted to visualise his internal organs and mentally change the relations they had with each other.

He missed making his own meat but he didn't miss his wife Halina. She had left the homeland rashly by train to go west. 'I have too much religion', she said to him when they first met one summer in a minimart in Kilburn, in the hope he would absolve her. 'I have strange ideas about marriage', he replied. Neither thing bothered the other because they were so much in love. When they married these two very same things became the absolute focus of separate existences and they descended into dreary domestic wrangling. She tried her hand at different jobs, but always came back to the comfort of Polish minimarts, whereas he trained as a gasman in northern provincial towns, making his own meat from the numerous parks and hills that counted for geography. This, if nothing else, was approved by his wife, who could see God's order in the killing of non-human species. His idea of marriage was more religious than hers, a surprise to her but not to him, because he had always felt the need to be uxorious, to have a different way of being his self, as if being a husband would liberate him from who or what he had been before, since that was the self that bored him. She immersed herself in *Dekalog*, and although he avoided it he couldn't escape dreaming scenes of adultery and coveting and idolatry and state retribution and living in Polish flats. A close-up of the lawyer who failed to save the young murderer from legal hanging haunted him, emerging from his car into the field of lost childhood to scream 'I abhor it, I abhor it'. Now this was the it to be abhorred. The gasman's only release from the insinuations of the films was doing what he loved most, going into other people's houses without being obliged to stay there, the one activity the other side of ennui, reading numbers underground, tracing in his mind's eye the path of gas as it moved vast distances through the Atlantic to make ovens and fires glow, believing in the corporate magic that held the network together, as if God had planned it all along to be just this way and no other. Being locked in a cellar was his Fate, which he soon embraced: it was time to commit to one house, the Fate of all gasmen. He had no abiding interest in electricity. 'I abhor it, I abhor it', he screamed back when asked about noises in an attic he would never see, a place he imagined as the Kingdom of Poland in miniature, with the incarcerating man and woman sufficient to play all the actors in all the films in all the apartments. He watched the dial measure the flow of gas from the Atlantic, mentally and spiritually reducing the height of all the seas in all the world as he did so.

What most impressed the gasman was the way his liberation from domesticity had been so carefully planned by the ambitious young couple overhead. In the cellar was a mess, a mess carefully arranged for him to start rebuilding his life in any way he saw fit. When one morning after many mornings the fascination of the dials wore off he turned his attention to the large mound of earth which the builders had failed to clear some hundred years ago. It doubled up as a meteorite and sometime bees' nest from which he could garner honey. The shadow of visitors to other houses continued to project into the cellar through the small barred window and onto the chaos and mound which were gradually taking shape into a telling new world. Why did nobody try to save him? Perhaps his wife had accepted her widow fate as it had been coded into the *Dekalog*. Perhaps she had remarried, chosen a priest this time, or the opposite of priests. These days his mind wandered and he scarcely considered how his internal organs were to be rearranged and how he was to become the other gasman. He needed to retrain his mind. As he remembers it from Genesis, all his cells and tissue and neuronal activity are just like the other man's. This is the easy part though.

The Phenomenology of Shit

1.1

Just to recap, I've unfortunately been made the literary executor of Johannes Boanerges, one of the most prominent and important philosophers of the twentieth and early twenty-first centuries. Unfortunate because there's so much of his writing still in its raw state and it will mean a lifetime's work – *my* lifetime – to put in order the papers of my old friend and nemesis. What is worse, if you remember, is that I have to go through Victor(ia), his whatever (cook, cleaner, amanuensis, lover, gender tester) to access materials that are referred to in the papers I have but which don't seem to exist. A cynic might suspect that they never did exist, such were his game-playing antics and fitful anti-academic anti-philosophical stance, but I take the optimist's path and know that if I look hard enough I will uncover them. This cannot be a world lost to us, for if these works are lost to us, seemingly more important (even more important, I should say) than the works we have, civilisation is doomed (a half-jest). Obviously I have my own work to get on with, and get on with it I will, yet there is also the painful sense of ethical obligation to JB.

I had put off contacting Victor(ia) for months in order to do my own work, thinking it best to work out the best means of putting the Boanerges house in order by letting it bubble away in my subconscious and sleep patterns, rather than approaching the problem head-on and using my own brain space for the dead philosopher's benefit. A bit of a shock then to receive a phone call from him or her, himer (from now on), asking me to go to the house because shehe (from now on) had discovered something of hiser master's that shehe thought I should see.

Johannes lived in a mansion in a run-down part of the city, and I was not surprised to see all sorts of detritus littering the areas inside the privet and inside the fence once I'd eased myself through the unshut but stuck wrought-iron gates. God, I thought, if *I* can devote time to clearing up Johannes's philosophical litter the least *shehe* can do is to clear up the material stuff. Or did shehe think shehe was too elevated in the world after receiving the majority of JB's inheritance. When shehe came to the door shehe looked no different from hiser time before as whatever, and to be absolutely fair (why not?) to himer it was the gardener's job to look after the grounds. They weren't the most extensive that could be imagined. When I pointed this out to himer shehe said that it had all been cleared last week by a gardener and that what I had seen represented a few days material disgruntlement from the community who had come to mildly dislike the celebrity in their midst (a couple of appearances on national television to denounce injustice). There had been no trickle-down effect in the last two decades of his residence, in which they assumed him to be as rich as Abramovic, and any words of sympathy that might have been associated with the impoverished locals were at such a philosophically abstract level it was difficult to eat them or warm yourself with them, or even keep yourself amused while you were deprived elsewhere of material comfort. There was a preponderance of used condoms, so in some sense all was not lost since the young ones at least abused the memory of my good friend with some thoughts of the future. It occurs to me, given youth's natural tendencies, that what is about to unfold will be both use and ornament.

Yes, Victor(ia) looked no different from whenever, dressed in a butlermaid's mourning weeds, and closed the large front-door behind me. Shehe wasn't exactly solicitous, but nor was shehe as exactly hostile as shehe was when I was first engaged in extracting as much of the great man's legacy in manuscript form from hiser hands. Shehe offered to make me a drink of tea or coffee, or even give me something stronger, but I declined all three in case they were poison. Shehe was not offended, went into what used to be Johannes's study, and returned with a large sealed manila envelope, not particularly bulky, but with something that was more than a couple of sheets of paper. The envelope was addressed to Johannes at the address I was standing in, with a postmark 4 April 1985 and sent from this area. Victor(ia) explained that hiser master used to post copies of his work to himself for copyright reasons (if there were any challenge, he could simply produce the sealed, dated envelope). It was an old, pointless trick, and in any case, who could ever doubt the authenticity of his work? His style was *sui generis*. My God! I knew Johannes had his little anxieties, as do we all, but it never occurred to me that he believed the authenticity of his work could ever be in doubt. The man questioned the nature of authenticity with great authenticity! What was worse, of course, was that I, as his friend and literary executor, should have known that Johannes operated this system. How could I not know? I looked at Victor(ia) steadily with my old mistrust, cursing Johannes for putting me at this person's mercy. It was beginning to look more and more like a joke on his part played upon his old friend.

'Any more?' Shehe shook her head. I asked himer again. Was shehe smiling behind hiser implacable visage? 'Any more?'

'This is the only envelope'.

That didn't make sense. If Johannes was so paranoid as to use this system to prove copyright, there must be hundreds of the things. My heart sank again. How many more times would this business of literary executor bring me down? Yet I didn't know what was in this envelope. Why hadn't Johannes written on the outside what the inside contained? Surely he had a system.

'Where are the others?'

'There are no others'.

'I have to go to the toilet', I said.

'Upstairs, turn . . .'

'I know where the toilet is, thank you very much'.

I'd completely forgotten where the upstairs toilet was and wandered into a closet, which I quickly exited, only to find myself in what I took to be Victor(ia)'s bedroom. I didn't linger (honest) because what I really wanted to do was open the envelope as soon as possible as well as go to the toilet, my plumbing not being what it used to be. The truth is, these days, little trickles have started to materialise, and whether this is a dicky bladder or irritable bowel syndrome I can't say and am too embarrassed to go to the doctor's for fear I will have to wear a big nappy-like appendage.

I could have left the envelope with Victor(ia) downstairs since shehe was hardly going to do anything with it now having voluntarily put it into my hands, and things would go swifter without having to care for the precious cargo while I engaged in micturation. Coming back to me as I wandered lost on the landing was the disposal of the toilets. There was one in the bathroom, I recalled, and one by itself, which I found first and went in desperately. The room was very small, just sufficient space to turn round, but the door wouldn't shut properly. A quaint old latch placed into a hook was the only means of securing the door. Who would storm in and surprise me? The ghost of Joho? There was no reading matter provided, which always annoys me, since I like to be using my time profitably all the time, when I remembered the envelope (how could I forget?) and this presented me with something of a behavioural dilemma. Micturation could only plausibly give me two or three minutes, and I couldn't very well open the envelope and read it while micturating. Defecating, on the other hand, could plausibly give me a good fifteen minutes reading time, with just the social embarrassment of facing Victor(ia) in the knowledge that this is what I 'had been up to' ('What have you been doing?' 'I have been . . .'). It wouldn't have been a problem in the days when Joho was alive, we were relatively free and easy about these things, but times had changed and I had to move with the times. JB was dead and Victor(ia) had inherited everything other than the manuscripts (subject to the obligatory challenge from one of Johannes's offspring – another inheritance story). It was as if the house were now new to me, and I a first-time visitor, and social etiquette is clear that you cannot defecate in a house on a first visit, although how many visits are required is nowhere specified. Damn it! There was nothing for it except to sit and read and to brave Victor(ia)'s reproof. So sit I did. I should say that I had no intention of actually engaging in the act of defecation, only this I knew is what a fifteen-minute break would give Victor(ia) the impression of.

I dropped my trousers and pants and settled myself down for a good quarter-of-an-hour in the company of the envelope's contents, which amounted to twelve pages of typescript on flimsy paper, and which I've rendered here in a similar typeface to give you the same experience. Sitting comfortably? I was.

The Phenomenology of Shit
by
Johannes Boanerges

I saw Susie sitting in a shoe shine shop.
Where she sits she shines,
and where she shines she sits.

I have never considered myself to be a phenomenologist, retreating, monk-like, into the meanderings of my consciousness to seek out the essence of the appearance of reality as it appears to me. I have never sought that kind of knowledge. Edmund Husserl, in his Cartesian Meditations (two lectures delivered in German in 1929, published in French in 1931) says we must, as philosophers, at some point in our lives jettison everything we already know and start from scratch to build up a philosophy brick by brick, accounting for each brick. We must adopt the phenomenological approach to effect this, we must 'bracket out' the objects we seek to understand. Indeed, it is very much like a meditation, and the object of meditation can be anything: 'love', 'existence', 'a tree'. He shows us how to remove all preconceptions of the object of our enquiry; this act of removal takes us to the heart, the essence of the object. Heidegger considers 'being' using this method, Sartre considers gas lamps and lemons (and then, o.k., ~~his overweening ugly self~~ being). Thus, an important philosophical carriage gets under way and phenomenology rules the world, a new

73

science. Hooray -- philosophy that is also science.

From the title of this ~~essay~~ book you will know already what I am going to say next, for you are an intelligent reader and understand these things. If phenomenology is our entry to

Page Two

greater understanding of everything there is in the universe, then it is only right we apply this method to everything there is in the universe. From trees and lemons to the quiddity of our own existence, the phenomeno-logical method gives us the precise character of our thisness, our here-and-nowness, that we crave as human beings. And Levinas and some others using the very same method, give us the essence of our relationships, and these ~~two too~~ are also important. Why then, and you know what's coming now and what cannot be avoided because I've told you it already in the title and you didn't want to believe that this is really what I am going to talk about did you?, why then do the great and good of philosophy not meditate upon the nature of shit? It falls to me, to Johannes Boanerges, who has nothing to fear from the groves of philosophical academe, to think about the brown stuff, and discourse on its nature and signi-ficance at length.

This is not a frivolous undertaking ('honest', as a good English friend of mine would say), not frivolous at all. Husserl takes us back

74

to Descartes and his method of doubt. Husserl is in thrall (?) to the Cartesian 'I think therefore I am', the fact that he thinks is proof of his existence against all else. What a load of shit! Tons of the stuff!!! Cartesian, phenomenological shit!!!!!!!!

Does anybody, in all seriousness, doubt that they exist? Do you? And, really!!!!, would sitting at home doubting you exist be overcome because you realised only somebody who existed could doubt their existence? Is this really the sum of ~~Western philosophical thought~~ it all? What monstrous egos those Cartesian philos- ophers have (Note: Husserl – 'transcendental ego'). Do you need to kick a stone and feel the pain to know that you exist?

This is off the point. Let's stick to seeing the world as it is, stripping away our prejudices and getting to the

Page Three

essence of everything. That truly would be a science! Husserl, and every other philosopher, they use nice examples, they really do. We're going to use a not-nice example, shit. Why don't they (philosophers, scientists, nice people) use shit? It is part of the world, is it not? Not polite? Should we let politeness get in the way of seeing the world as it is? Here begins my beschissen Untersuchungen, my own phenomeno- logical investigation into shit.

I begin by keeping a diary, recording the

sensations involved and the thoughts around those sensations. In order to meditate I must bracket out all I know of shit, strip away those prejudices. Please, follow me! And what do I know of shit? I excrete, therefore I . . . If I don't excrete I die. I must not be shitty, have shit in me. Yet all the time there is shit in me, I make shit all the time. Even lingering over a meal the food cannot be in my mouth for many seconds whereas my body spends hours, days, making shit. At any given moment my body-weight, my BODY, is made of the thing I wish it not to be made of. Be gone, shit! And yet, I am shit, the thing I wish not to be. Is it time to think again about shit (were we thinking of it before?)? This is not the phenomenological method. I cannot replace one ideology of shit with another for this is not the removal of prejudice but the substitution of prejudice. I need to think nothing about shit before thinking about shit afresh. All the hatred for the stinking steaming mess my body creates anew must go. My body creates what it must reject. My body is a paradox. Existence is a paradox. The food in England! It begins as shit! Pah! That is something else. Imagine beautiful food turned to shit. My body homogenises the natural world, turns the whole world brown.

This is not philosophy. This is random writing. Is this phenomenology? Is phenomenology ordered? Should I let my mind ramble without structure, like this? Is this shit? When I think shit, I am shit? Am I shit whether I think about being shit, or am I only shit when I consider it? Shit.

The diary. What I need to record is everything to do with shit to get to the essence of shit, and since I am evidently designed to create it (see above) we should be getting at something important overlooked by all previous philosophers. Thus, and only thus, will we understand the nature of our existence. Only the human has the capacity to contemplate its shit.

JOHANNES BOANERGES'S LOG

Day One

Sat down on the toilet. Tried to meditate but couldn't do it. I'm hopeless at this sort of thing, always have been. Should I give up now on the first day? I want to give up now. It's going to be too hard to do. I'm a natural quitter.

While I was trying, thinking very hard how to clear my mind, I barely noticed that my bowels had cleared themselves. There is an unpleasant smell is all I can record here. It's a start. (Do I need to record wiping my bottom, flushing? Is this part of the meditation?)

Day Two

I am not writing the actual dates of my toilet
visits down, as you may have noticed, just in
case you wanted to simultaneously act out what
I'm doing (comparing our diaries: 'mess observation'). If we are lucky we shit every day.
It is a timeless activity. It is a universal
activity. It is not specific to any time or
place. There is not a human who hasn't ~~shitted~~
shat, ergo we cannot be human without shitting and without being shit. This is our common
denominator~~?~~.

Day Three

Page ~~Four~~ Five

Just when I ~~was~~ am getting in the mood,
thinking of Husserl, thinking of shit, there
is a shout to tell me Knut is here. *Shittus
interuptus*. Knut is a shit. He will bore me
to death with his latest truth statement.
'"It is raining" or "It is not raining",
Johannes, it cannot be both. From this we
can proceed to truths about the world'. I
tell him of the time I was standing at the
top of a hill overlooking a 'Pitch and Put'
(Note to self: is that what they are called?)
between Torquay and Paignton in Devon where
I was forced to take my holidays as a child
when we visited England. Where I stood on
the hill it was not raining, but two hundred
yards away I could see a cloud with rain

78

descending on the golfing fathers, as if the whole scene ~~were~~ was a cartoon (a bad day for fathers with the dark cluster of clouds following them around, directly above their heads, attached by God, moving with them into caravans, tents and chalets much to the consternation of long-suffering suburban housewives. English humour). It is raining and not raining <u>at the same time</u>. From this we can proceed to something else, some other more important truths, perhaps the holidays in England when I was forced to visit Devon, and my first love-falling there.

Day Four

Is it fair to call Knut a shit? He is doing his best with limited talents, like so many of his fellow philosophers, so many of these great thinkers who refuse to think about shit. If shit is common to all humans, if it is the thing we can never escape for 'we make as we evacuate', it is perhaps the one thing (at last!) that can form the basis of democracy. Hah! Hurrah!!! What is Norwegian philosophy, Knut? (Note: unfair?)

Day Five

Page Five

I do not think I have been straining hard enough at this phenomenological reduction. I am sitting down and trying harder, which also means not forcing it out. It is both the act of shitting and the shit itself. Or should it be one or the other? Which is it, Edmund? And should I not think of people as shits? This is a prejudice, a connection, in particular in relation to Knut, which has occurred to me only since I began meditating and stripping out the prejudices I previously had, so it is part of my new understanding.

This is much harder than I thought, and still, no closer to the essence of shit than when I started.

Day Six

Constipated.

Day Seven

Constipated.

Day Eight

Strong laxative. Pain. Lots of toilet. Don't really want to think about it. My God! The watery inconsistency. Is this what shit can be like as well? I have not experienced it before, in all the years I have lived, so it is a completely new experience for me. So many different manifestations? It's like shit, but isn't shit? It has no solidity, it is liquid waste. Do we need a taxonomy of stools? I wish I had measured the number, size, consistency, colour, time of . . ., time to . . ., feelings about . . ., thoughts of . . ., memories of . . .

Day Nine

Page Seven

Normal shitting resumed. Having failed over more than a week to enter my consciousness of shit and shitting I have brought
with me Husserl's *Ideas* to help me along. Section 35: 'Let us begin with examples. Lying in front of me in the semi-darkness is this sheet of paper'. (Italians learning English struggle with the pronunciation of vowels: 'ship' or 'sheep', 'shit' or 'sheet'. Beside the point). 'Let us begin with examples. Lying beneath me (now) is this bowl of shit. I am seeing it, touching it'. Oh dear. Does Edmund really want me to touch it, or just to touch it 'with my mind?' There is his paper in front of me, and my shit underneath, which I can see when I peer between my legs but am loathe to touch. Should I touch it, for the sake of philosophy?

Descartes' Meditation Six (Modified)

'I possess a distinct idea of shit, inasmuch as it is only an extended and unthinking thing, it is certain that this shit . . . is entirely and absolutely distinct from my body, yet I cannot exist without it'

We despise the shit. We need the shit.

Shit and Ethics

I've given up on the log. A phenomenology of shit is not possible by direct(ion) so I will come at it indirectly. What happens when we bring shit and ethics together? Is it possible for them to shine a light on each other? Is it possible to have 'a good shit' or 'to be a good shit'?

Page Eight

Heidegger, the good German, treated his teacher, Husserl, a German Jew, like shit, once the Nazis got under way. Stole all his ideas and then abandoned him. Heidegger's philosophy is not one abounding in ethics. Is phenomenology? Only if we consider the essence of shit. Perhaps this is what Husserl always had in mind. From memory, Luther: 'Jews are full of the devil's faeces which they wallow in like swine'. The whole history of Christianity is this abiding hatred then: 'the Jews are full of shit'. It is possible to understand the engine of European history for four hundred years through this simple equation.

Can this be right? Should I forget this when using the phenomenological method? Should I forget the

The rest of this page has been torn off, and there are five pages to read and three problems emerge, one editorial, one practical, and one poetic-philosophical. Perhaps four problems: the intersection of phenomenology and ethics. Perhaps five problems: the tension between history and philosophy, between 'what was' and 'what is', between 'what was' and 'what ought to be'.

I hope you haven't forgotten that I'm sitting on the toilet as if a first-time guest and, without prompting, have done some business. JB doesn't record wiping, 'finishing off' as he called it (yes, as I said, we were free and easy about these things), and this is the position I find myself in. I am done and need to finish the business. There is no toilet paper. I look around. The room is small, a toilet only, no cupboards for back-up. If I can't see a toilet roll, then there isn't one. There's nothing in the roll holder and nothing on the top of the cistern. I would give my children one piece of advice only in life: 'Before shitting, check for paper'. The only paper I have is Johannes Boanerges' unpublished essay on phenomenology, now, in my hand. I hear Victor(ia) shout: 'Knut is here! Please finish toilet; come down'. (Shehe speaks perfectly good English when shehe wants to, so I don't know what's going on here. What game is shehe playing?) 'Knut says it is important, he must speak now, he's in a hurry – he hurries'. Hisher voice pierces the house, a weird counter-tenor affair that makes me shiver. Have I met Knut before, the serious bore? I wonder if he knows about JB's phenomenological project. Is Victor(ia) trying out for musical theatre? Shehe nearly sings the operatic state-of-play to make sure the audience can keep up.

There's no paper to wipe my arse, only the 'Phenomenology of Shit', which may be a masterpiece. Really, I can't use the essay, can I? Victor(ia) shout-sings up again to hurry. 'It's now or never' she arias, not a phrase I've heard her sing before. It must be Knut's who perhaps has a very good grasp of idiomatic English. 'Now or never!' I visualise what's happening at the bottom of the stairs. Too polite, of course, the both of them, to come up the stairs. I have established that I cannot – simply cannot – use 'The Phenomenology of Shit' to finish off, it must be preserved at all costs. I am reluctant to stand up without knowing the exact state of *mon derrière*. Does some matter cling? What does Joho say, what practical advice in the very chapter which deals with the very substance, the very essay that placed me in this predicament? Nothing! 'Hurry up! Hurry up! Hurry up!' Shehe definitely is singing now. I visualise what is happening at the bottom of the stairs and convince myself that if I open the door they will not be able to see me. There is nothing else for it – I am thinking as clearly as I ever have done in my life in a stressful situation – and carefully placing the papers on the floor close to the door, I stand up and turn round.

I stare into the toilet bowl. It is of the German model with a shelf to collect the stools for close observation before consignment to sewage (I know – only the Germans. One of Joho's identity strands). There isn't much water in the toilet and I peer down to see just how much and, in a way, to see how much I can avoid looking at my own shit. There in the puddle is my face, calm I would like to think even as Victor(ia)'s song drifts up imploringly – 'Help, it's Knut, he's in a hurry' (repeated; this must be the chorus) – and no surprises, there it is, my ugly mug, the Face of the Same. At the very least, it can't smell what I can smell (I presume).

Why is there hardly any water in the toilet? 'Hurry up, it's time! Knut awaits!' I will flush and then with fresh toilet water I will clean my bottom, dry as best I can, and return to civilisation, such as it is in the shape of a hermaphroditical servant (I am convinced now that Victor(ia) can generate hiser own offspring, another train of thought I had while reading JB's essay) and a tedious Knut. I flush and nothing happens, no water comes to clean away the mess I'm in. I flush again and again, but it's dry flushing, and even though I am convinced nobody will rush the stairs and burst in, I start to realise that I may be in a bit of a pickle, standing staring at the rejection of what was me, now formatted differently and taking it easy on stained porcelain. Adamant.

A strange calculation enters my head, part of the strange plan my subconscious has formulated throughout the whole time I have been focussed on another matter, a plan that I have tried to suppress because it can only end in tears. Or will it? I am thinking clearly now, after all is said and done. Haven't I stood up without mishap? That's an encouraging start. The calculation: there is a window of opportunity for me to gather up the shit in my two hands, run across the landing to the toilet in the bathroom, deposit it in the proper toilet there, flush with water that will appear as it should, wipe my arse with the proper toilet paper that's there in the bathroom, pull up my pants and trousers, and wash my hands and dry them on the towel, just like normal people do every day. 'Come down, Knut is here, hurry, Knut is here,

Knut is here, Knut is . . .' The calculation: only one trip can be made – will all the waste matter fit in my hand in one go? You know, it's crazy, but I think it might just work! I won't be able to run – I can't take the risk of pulling up my pants on to an unwashed *derrière* – skidmarks and worse – but a fast shuffle across the landing to the sanctuary of a proper bathroom, flushing water, toilet paper, soap, fluffy towel, should suffice.

'Come! Come! The plumber is come!'

(Bass) 'Where is the problem? What is the problem? Can you count them? Can we count them?'

That makes sense.

Is that good or bad?

It's now or never. Victor(ia) sings up: 'Descend! Descend!' Hiser voice ascends the mansion to this small troubled room, in a descending florid chromatic motif, a counterpoint to the bass. Knut, a tenor, 'I'm in a hurry / Time moves slow / I sure do worry / It's time to go' battles against the others. What to do? What to do? It's all crowding in on me, at the very moment when I thought my mind was clear. Descend, hurry, plumbing. All we need is a fourth voice, a soprano. And there it is! I have no idea who, but it's beautiful, soaring, resonant with the counter-tenor, bass, tenor, and yet holding a distinctive timbral range. And what is she singing if not 'Johannes! Boanerges!'

All the problems appear simultaneously just at the moment when I thought I had cleared my mind. Everything, *everything* at once. Can I think everything at once? There is no time to lose. I put my hands either side of the shit on the shelf and scoop it up, it's not as bad as I thought it would be, though pretty bad, let's be honest, and barge the door open and shuffle at speed across the landing, 'Descend', 'time moves slow / I sure do worry', 'The plumber', 'What is the problem?', fencing with each other downstairs and in my head. One of the voices isn't pitch-perfect and I'm desperate to shout down and point this out. It's the plumber, I'm sure. It's so hard to get professional singing plumbers these days. Joho said as much. Can they see me? An elderly man with the heart of a sixty-year old, skiffling as fast as his scrawny legs will go and the trousers and pants shackling his ankles will allow, carrying the recently released contents of his bowels? Can they see me? *Can they?*

Yes, they can. The singing stops. I look down. They look up. I crouch behind the banister rail. The spindles are ridiculously narrow. Why spend so much time crafting narrow banister spindles that will never in a million years hide a naked man crouching and holding his own shit? Why? To regain some dignity I stand up straight – I'm not going to hide. Hasn't the great Johannes now lifted the discourse of shit to a higher, philosophical level? Can't I display the brown stuff with pride? I think I can, and move up against the rail, holding my hands well out in front of me (holding back vomit – my God, the stench, the sticky brown adherence), and sing!, 'Look, what I have here!' There is a vagrant, and it is she who has the ethereal soprano, and takes up her line again, 'Jo–*hannes*! Bo–*aner*–ges!' The others join in with their well-rehearsed parts. I'm a success (but why don't they sing *my* name?)! Johannes is a success. Smiles all around!!! I take my time now, bow twice, and with grandeur proceed to the bathroom with my shit, having proved my self.

1.2

'Where are the sheets that you gave me?'

'The shits? I don't understand. You take the shits into the other room. I tell you, I try to tell you, pipes are bad in small toilet room, toilet not working, but you run up the stairs and don't listen. You never listen to me. You don't like me'.

'When I got back into the small toilet room the envelope and the essay in the envelope were gone. You and those three idiots were stood around. One of you took the chapter back. It is a work of genius. I can reconstruct some of it from memory, but I don't want to. I suppose I will have to. *Why did you take it? You stupid man-woman, you stupid I don't know what*. You are ruining my life. I am spending all this time putting Johannes's literary work in order and you obstruct me at every turn. It's *your* fault I had to carry my own shit. And now this. It was all for nothing, nothing. I'm at my wit's end'.

'Do not cry. The soprano took it? We will find her. Let us go and find her'.

'I can't reconstruct that essay . . . I *must*. It is a revelation. It is a new way of thinking and I must show the world or the world will be lost. I am convinced'.

'He was a genius I do not understand. What did it say?'

We begin to relax with each other, bracketing out our petty personal hatreds thanks to the healing power of JB's thought. We are in the study, sat in the two great tattered red leather armchairs, smoking cigars, drinking brandy at three in the afternoon, the cold sun streaming through, dust motes serendipitously forming perfectly legible sentences that are gone in a puff, to reconvene in some other language. Is Victor(ia) beginning to resemble JB? Have I been wrong about himer all this time? Her English cracks like Joho's every now and then, and she has begun to spin out phrases, thoughts, radical ideas, paradoxes. Shehe asks me what the essay was about and I tell himer. Shehe laughs. Shehe's all right, you know?

'Where is the essay?' Shehe laughs. I repeat the question. Shehe laughs, as if not understanding a word single word that I am saying or have said. I go over to himer, jabbing the cigar in hiser direction, playfully, then in a more sinister fashion, running the whole gamut of cigar gestures yet besieged by nonce words popping into my head which are irrelevant, a trick of the mind when I am trying hard to focus on the matter in hand. 'Where is the essay?' Victor(ia) goes back to being Victor(ia), my fault, I suppose, for breaking the mood and the trust. There can be no trust where Victor(ia) is concerned. Trust is not something that can be turned on or off, can it?, trust is something that is there or not there. 'I don't trust you', I say, 'where is the essay on shit?'

'I don't have the sheets. I have my other problems'.

'Are you saying "shit" or "sheet"?'

'You must leave this house and never come back. I am a servant. You have the papers, all of them. There are no more papers. My problems'.

'Spare me'.

It's true that I was now sat back in the armchair, enjoying my time through a brandy fug, taking the turn of events in a light-hearted manner, much to my own surprise, and it was no stretch to imagine JB and Victor(ia) sparring in just this manner. Shehe rolled up the right trouser leg — baggy trousers, hiding a multitude, no doubt — and pointed towards the middle of the shin where a small area glistened in the sunlight. From the position I was sat it was not possible to make out the cause of the shine.

'What is it?'

'Bone. It is bone'.

'Oh, it is shin bone'.

'Sheen? Leg bone? No, it looks like tooth bone'.

'Did something bite you and leave a bit of tooth in there?'

Then it occurred to me – why hadn't I thought of it before? Victor(ia) had manufactured that essay, perhaps from Johannes' ideas, and re-using an old envelope had faked the whole thing.

'Did you write "The Phenomenology of Shit", Victor, open bracket "ia", close bracket?'

'I have my legs problem. Why won't you look at my legs problem?'

'I am not a doctor' (which wasn't true – I had qualified as a doctor – another story I told only JB). 'Yes, you have a tooth in your leg, who would have thought it? So what? You have the kind of fleshiness that can accommodate such extraneous matter. See your doctor. Did you write the essay? Did you copy it out? How much of it is you? How much of it is Johannes? What have you done with it? It is *very very very* important'.

'What is "pho . . . no . . . gy"?'

If you strangle a revolting servant, does the world pay heed? She was smiling, pretending not to be able to pronounce the word, making an ass of me. I needed to go to the toilet again and told her as much. The brandy made me unsteady when I got up, everything rushing in to my head, and she quickly came to me, and in return for help I looked at the glossy white item in her leg, which did indeed look like a very small bone chip half-submerged in a sea of redness. 'I wouldn't worry about it – these things happen' and clambered up to the toilet. The whole leg was puffy and marbled. Perhaps the essay would miraculously reappear, just as whole pages had begun to appear in the dust that followed me out of the study. Perhaps the essay would appear like this, in the ether, a sign from JB from beyond the grave. Perhaps I didn't need the essay – it could be written in this manner. I started paying more attention to the dust, for it followed me into the bathroom like Devon rainclouds above families on holiday that rain and don't rain simultaneously. Each time I attempted to hold on to the words and the ideas new ones came along and pushed the old ones out before they could be fixed (which is why I am not able to put anything down here). Was this dust the dust of Johannes? It was *his* house, so it was conceivable that the dust had the memory of its philosopher-owner ingrained and it was also conceivable that even according to the logic of chaos some order would be established that could aid the reformation of the thoughtful dust of Johannes. If only JB could give me a proper sign rather than these ambiguous mini-marvels I thought standing up taking a piss, which was proving to be more painful than usual. At least there was no blood in the dark urine. Blood from a nether orifice was what I most feared at my age, a sign of the inevitable. Victor(ia) sang up to me, rhyming 'right' with 'tight' (as in 'bladder is tight') in such a beautiful melody that its nonsensical nature passed me by. I sang back that 'I am all right / in this world of moths and rust / as right as right can be / when all must turn to dust'. If I were to stay longer, I would develop this motif slyly introducing my former meditation on 'trust'. It wasn't a libretto I was prepared to devote time to beyond these four walls. Perhaps Victor(ia) did care for me in some small way as hiser main link to Johannes, as I did for himer. Was it time to trust the servant? I rehoused the offensive item and made my way back downstairs. The envelope had reappeared, but without the essay.

'Please, look at my other leg'. I understood, perfectly. Shehe went behind the chair and adjusted hiser clothing, put himerself back in the chair with bare feet – shehe must have removed hiser thick tights – and pulled up the heavy black pleated skirt which shehe had changed into while I was in the toilet to reveal a leg that looked like shit, with three molars emergent on the top of the upper thigh and an incipient eye just below the knee. Victor(ia) signalled with a clever glance that I should look behind and peer into the knee pit and there to my real astonishment was a fully-formed eye, blinking into the light out from the dark hollow, even winking at me or pleading for release. I understood, perfectly. Here it was then that the servant continued to suffer. Had shehe understood more than Johannes? Had I been looking in the wrong place? Had Victor(ia) had a hand in typing 'The Phenomenology of Shit'? Had shehe understood more than Johannes ever could?

Believing me to be in a state of shock, I was led by hand into Victor(ia)'s bedroom, given a skirt, tights, a woman's wig and some dark lipstick (which didn't suit my skin colour *at all*), and guided to the park to recover. It was here we stood outside a well-maintained toilet block on a cold spring day, blustery here, there, and everywhere, cherry blossom driving into our faces to compensate for the stern, immoveable, unkillable, unlikeable, laurel bushes that embraced the brickwork. There was a small crowd of humanity waiting close to the female entrance, eyes on a clump of trees at the top of a hill. A well-dressed middle-aged woman emerged, pulling a suitcase behind her, walking with elegant purpose towards us. As she got closer there was an awful smell and I silently indicated the presence of a stink to Victor(ia) who made out that I should not draw attention to it. The crowd parted and the woman and the stink went inside the toilet block, and also let Victor(ia) and myself through into the women's, not noticing I was a man dressed as a woman, even with my wig slipping and the wrong choice of lipstick self-evident, and not suspecting Victor(ia)'s gender indeterminacy. Out of the suitcase came tin cans, some still with their labels on, and the source of the smell. How I didn't gag I don't know – perhaps politeness conquers all. There were human faeces in each can, which Victor(ia) helped take out of the suitcase, and when you looked inside each piece of shit formed itself into an imploring human face, crying out from the depths. The human waste was scraped from tin to toilet with the crowd looking on, awed by the woman's dignity. Each emptied can was wordlessly handed to Victor(ia) who placed it on the sink and began to clean with rags provided by the woman. I was worried that people would discover I wasn't a female and shouldn't be there, but the woman and Victor(ia) were distraction enough for the small crowd of humanity, and anyway, there were some men in the audience as well who hadn't come in drag. I could hear a group of Spanish students outside being hushed by the believers who stood on the threshold guarding the entrance. In turn the students of foreign culture too became fully awed and convinced a group of elderly Chinese men (I really could hear that far) behind them of the significance of the event. Truly now was the time for 'The Phenomenology of Shit' to be scraped into the world, for we had arrived at the very juncture Johannes and Victor(ia) had foreseen, the very moment in our history when we could understand its meaning perfectly.

Zeroth

With my head on the pillow looking toward the window the edge of the duvet is very large in my line of sight. Very large. Nearly the whole picture.

The edge of the duvet. Not very important.

I could get up now. Pretend it's a quarter-past five in the afternoon, not in the morning. Deceive myself.

Why haven't I moved? The edge of the duvet, with its yellow flowers and green leaves, is not fascinating. The perspective I have lying here is not fascinating in the least little bit. I need sleep. I don't care if I never wake up. Mark One in the States. Fact.

In the midst of morning Clar contemplates her empty brilliance. My empty brilliance. Fact. Truth value = 1. With my hand on the pillow looking toward the window the edge of the duvet, with its yellow flowers and green leaves and low tog rating because of the superior central heating we installed when the girls were young, is very large in my line of sight and I am emptily brilliant. Very large.

The edge of the duvet. Note, not very important.

I'm o.k. now but I'll be very tired later on, too tired to make important decisions. I should cancel the meeting with Azad and Chloe.

I could get up now. Pretend it's a quarter past five in the afternoon, not the morning. Fool myself. I don't care if I never wake up. I should want to wake up.

There needs to be a field for wake-up. Question. Want to wake? Yes. No. Number. Date. Place. Husband Mark One. Home/Away. Daughter Number One. Home/Away. Issy. Daughter Number Two. Home/Away. Date. Place.

Get up. There cannot be a duvet field. There cannot be. It is not in the least way important. The duvet does not need to be captured. That would mean I have to capture everything. Data capture is structured, it is not a catch-all. Not everything is important. Certainly not the duvet large in my line of sight looking toward the window.

It wouldn't capture this feeling, not wanting to do anything.

Put a field into the Engine for not wanting to do anything, put in a field for feeling nothingness. Go on. Why not?

On the drive to the meeting the pink cherry blossom on the windscreen. Pink with brown edges, blowing away. End of April. Spring. Beyond the windscreen and spring nothing but empty fields. What was that feeling this morning? Put the windscreen wipers on. Do not put the windscreen wipers on.

That empty feeling. There all the time, not just mornings now. Not caring if I'm alive or dead. What is the name for that empty feeling there all the time? There needs to be a field for feelings with no names, with numerical markers. Start with the number one, not zero. That empty feeling. No, we have to start with zero.

0. It really has to be 0.

There have always been names for nothing. It is the number nothing which is special.

When is Mark One back from New York?

My feeling for Mark One is not zero, but it is not the feeling or collection of feelings I had in our first years together. Those feelings had names like lust and love and awe. My feeling for Mark one this April = 2.

The girls have drifted away. = 3.

Difficult to pinpoint. My love for them is tied up with what they used to be. They are other people now, their own selves. They are not with me, part of me, tied to me. I have a feeling when I think of them, individually or together, but I cannot name that feeling. = 4. Mark One + Feeling for Mark One + Girls have drifted away + Thinking of girls together and individually =.

Adds up to 0.

Other people have named 0 depression. I'm not depressed. Feeling nothing is depression though. No it's not. The feeling I have is.

0.

'Mother'. m0ther.

'Yes Clar'.

'Did Clarissa have a nervous breakdown? Is that what it is?'

'Clarissa who?'

'Clarissa Dalloway'.

'Of course she did'.

'Is that why she's always feeling "there", absolutely present to herself?'

'I don't understand you Clar. I haven't read that novel for the longest time, sweetness. I read Elizabeth Taylor now. That's what grown-up women read, novels about what it's like to be us, not women with psychological problems. I have to go'.

Why did dad hang himself in the garage?

= 5.

***

A field for dreams which must never by analyzed. Last night, the dream I remember from last night. I'm in Pakistan. Perhaps. Azad is there. The people are talking about a chicken shack. They put five chickens in there at a time at the beginning of each day. They don't kill them – there's a trapdoor or hole which they push them through – perhaps to kill them. When I see the shack it's the size of a shed. They open the door and it's crammed with chickens, but there are also people in there, rising above the chickens, women from the nineteenth century, not perturbed by their situation, and with little fuss heading to the door.

Dream Number 312. Record only. No cross-reference.

***

She blushed as Azad told her that the business had five thousand employees. The best way forward she told him would be for her to interview ten senior and twenty middle managers and look at their worksetting practices. It's a simple matter of inputting the number of hours up to their contracts, and assigning hours to tasks. She would meet the working party who were finalising hours-to-tasks.

'When I have done that, they will need to formulate a strategy for implementation and training. I know you wanted to take that phase in-house and retain my services on an ad-hoc basis, but I would again urge my involvement throughout the training and implementation phase. It's a false economy not to. You don't need a false economy'.

Clar continued to blush. Azad thought she was menopausal, having hot flushes like his mother.

***

Mark One wasn't there when she got back. She must have got the wrong day and wasn't motivated to clear up the inadequacy. She took the rosé out of the fridge and up to bed, got drunk and fell asleep, dreaming of her Engine.

***

The corner of the duvet with its cluster of yellow flowers and green leaves nearly took her eye out. Clar wondered how she felt. It wasn't immediately apparent on waking. The empty feeling rose within, a definite nothingness. She remembered the pink cherry blossom on the windscreen on the drive to the meeting, how the wind took it away. She remembered another detail from yesterday – white blossoms on trees in the fields. There was no such thing as a May tree. They are Hawthorns, she thought. Pointless thing to know. Her father used to point out trees and their names. 'Why did he hang himself in the garage?' My father used to point out the names of trees to me when I was a little girl, and then he hung himself in the garage.

***

Dream Number 313

My dream is of a car journey with a husband and children. The car is green, something like a Mini Cooper. I get the wrong turning off the dual-carriageway and calm down, thinking I know this road, it's from back home when I was

94

a teenager, before it changed. But I know it's not that road, and this road is twisting and turning. I know I'm not in complete control of the car, but convince myself that I am. It keeps shaping away sharply in dogs' legs and ahead there are fields and gravel pits. Nobody in the car is saying anything to me. They know I've taken a wrong turning and that sometimes I drive too fast when I'm in the wrong. I drive too fast so I don't have to think about the names of the trees. We go along these roads for quite a long time, the whole thing is irrelevantly picturesque, then the road straightens out and is going down fast, even though it doesn't seem that steep. I'm sure the brakes work because my brain isn't telling me any different, but all the same the brakes don't slow down the car, so they can't really be working. There's a large lake or pool straight ahead and I can carry on down the road towards it if I like, pressing the brakes, because the straight road does arc upwards towards the sky, like the end of a ski-slope, so that I know if I'm pushing on the brakes the car will come to a standstill at the top of the slope at the very least.

There are divergent roads either side of the water that I could take, but something tells me it would be a bad idea, that I would keep on with the endless car journey going in the wrong direction, being in the wrong, swerving left and right into dogs' legs. The car is heading for the end of the slope and I know the car is going to go straight into the water. I have to save myself, because it will be one less person to get out the sinking car, even though there are two children and my husband in there. I have to save myself.

I get out the car just as it flies off the end of the ski-slope into the water and stand watching it as it dives into the water, with the girl, the boy, and the man, my husband, my family, stuck inside it. There are people around the lake and one or two make for the car as quickly as possible. I stay where I am and then move slowly towards where the car sank, but I'm not wet yet. I don't see them get out the car, but they do escape and I'm really pleased that my daughter, aged between eight and ten, with her black hair flat against her face and head as if she's just been dragged up from the depths of the ocean, asks and cries for me, just for me, not for her father or her brother, and I hug her and cry.

This one man starts asking her why her daddy wasn't driving the car, although he doesn't say 'daddy', he says 'landlord', but he means her father. I'm scared they'll discover I bailed out and left the father and children to make their own way out of the car, and then they'll blame me and turn on me. (But who *was* driving the car? It doesn't make sense). I keep hugging my daughter, I love her so much, I really didn't know I could love her this much. But I'm sick with myself and can't understand why I was so pleased to see the girl first rather than the boy, since I thought I unconsciously favoured the boy over the girl. And I'm also puzzled as to why I'm not thinking about the father, although I am in fact calling him to mind in this way and thinking about him. I love them all so much that I don't understand why my love isn't every-where and at once and for all of the family and for all of the time.

Why is it separated out? The thought makes me feel more sick. The man keeps asking the question. His face isn't unkind. It's a little pock-marked, but I don't want this to sway my opinion of him. I just wished he wouldn't keep asking my daughter about why her father wasn't driving the car. Who does he think was driving the car?

End of dream Number 313

***

Dream Number 314.
There's a man in the house who appears to be called something like Dave Diamond, and I think he's here to teach my son to play the guitar. However, he isn't talking about what he's here for at all, he's just there, like he's one of the family, walking around in the living room. I can hear my husband in the kitchen clanking pans in a way which means it's up to me to entertain Dave Diamond, if that indeed is his name. He sort of ambles around the room, very relaxed, and me pretending to be relaxed and kind of nodding in agreement at something as if there is an unspoken connection between us, as if we both know what is going on. But I am definitely pretending, I don't really know what's going on, even if I'm sure Dave Diamond does. I have this vague thought that he's here to teach my son how to play the electric guitar. Because things often pop into my head like this and prove to be right, as if my memory clicks on by itself without telling me whether something I've remembered is right or not, as if the Engine is working without my control, which I think is quite possibly true.

I have to go in the kitchen then to see my husband. He carries on clanking pans. He knows about the man in the living room, but says nothing. He speaks through his attitude and says it's my problem to deal with, though I really don't remember personally inviting Dave Diamond in, I really don't. I say to the man that I suppose he's come to teach Matthew the guitar (I don't know if that is my son's name), and perhaps Matty isn't around because he's gone off the idea? Should I get Matty? But Josh (I don't know my husband's name either; it's not Josh, I just don't know what it is at all) still isn't interested and says that Dave Diamond has come the wrong week, it was last week(end) he should have come. I feel a bit better about the situation now that I have something definite to tell the guitar teacher, but part of me feels he won't be very happy to be told we don't want him to start teaching my son now.

In the same dream, and it's chronologically next, I'm on the bus going to Karen's, although I'm on the bus *with* Karen, so that doesn't make any sense, since I'm on the bus *to go and see her*. Bella is with us, and she's going to see Karen as well, *the same Karen*. The bus stops at the junction at the bottom of Karen's road and we get off and turn the corner into Karen's road where there's another bus stop. There's a crowd at the bus stop talking about the Engine and even though I tell Karen and Bella not to get on the bus because it's not far to walk to Karen's they get on it. I feel obliged to get on it as well, but they're not on it, which is annoying but seems to be part of the dream logic, so I don't worry too much, I feel I'm worrying just the right amount in the dream for a dream at this point. Also I'm not that worried because I can just get off at the next stop. So I do that, and Bella and Karen are already in Karen's house, which is surprising and a little annoying.
End of Dream Number 314

***

That reads like two separate dreams.
I am recording the dreams, but I won't put them in the Engine, I'm sure of that. The algorithms would determine the meaning but the algorithms would already be the meaning. You wouldn't need to read the dreams, only the algorithms. It would be a pointless exercise. 'We may say most aptly that the Analytical Engine weaves algebraical patterns just as the Jacquard-loom weaves flowers and leaves'. That may be so, but it does not weave from dreams. It weaves from the world around.

***

Dream Number 315.

It's early evening, dark, wet, and I'm standing on a bridge. Down below in the mud between the river and the bank, just beyond the foot of the bridge, there are police and other interested people. Somehow, unbidden, after minutes of waiting for this power, I can zoom in to where the focus of their attention is. The body emerging from the mud is his, after all these years, looking no different. There are no details, so perhaps he's just a skeleton, but in my heart I know it's him and that all the intervening years between then and now will be shown to have been a lie. I feel a sickness at the heart of me that hasn't been there in all the intervening years, and knowing I have lived without fear in those years as I've established myself with a husband and family makes me feel sicker. All those years they didn't know what I'd done, and I didn't know who I was myself. Now the horror of me is coming home. It was outside of me before, it must have been, I never felt it even if the murder was lodged in my brain as a fact. It's dark, and the slime and ooze and his body are all as one. I am sick of myself or at myself.

End of Dream Number 315.

When I wake up I feel sick like in the dream. I have no idea who the dead man was in the dream. Not anybody I know.

It's May now. The cherry blossom is mush in the driveway, indistinguishable from mud. They've called me back in for another meeting. I want to explain my holistic programming, and then perhaps Azad and Chloe will understand what I'm about, why I'm special. They don't need to know about Ada's language, they just need to know that it's the way I capture and process data that makes Clar Solutions the best.

The landscape is familiar from Dream 313, and I can drive as if in the dream, paying no attention to braking, gear-changes or indicating.

In the meeting Azad makes me blush ridiculously. I think my blushing makes him crimson too. They have accepted my argument, that is, the argument they should retain me throughout the implementation phase. The meeting is so short Chloe feels obliged to say something about her visit to New York. 'Ground Zero was so moving. To think . . .'

The Mayans had zero, but it didn't save them. They used it in their complicated calendar systems as a place-holder, but not for calculating things. It wasn't really a concept of zero, of nothingness. That's why they died out, they had no number to represent nothing so they had no intimation of the danger of their non-existence. All they could do was count the years in complicated calendar systems. Nobody knows why their sophisticated civilisation died out, but that's why. Nothing to do with failing to come up with the plough or steel. The failure to understand the power of 0 was their downfall. They used carved heads for zero. I wonder if Chloe saw Mark One at Ground Zero.

***

I go in to the Engine. I check the fields and their entries. I try out some different database queries. The results are ok but don't tell me anything new. I know what I have to do. I have to put zero into the Engine for it to make sense, I have to put the empty feeling in for it to tell me what is at the heart of things. How can I put nothingness into it?

***

Mark One says he will be back the weekend. It's wrong, I know, but I ask Azad out for a drink using an electronic communication. He doesn't reply. Perhaps he hasn't received it. I haven't the nerve to phone him directly. A dream comes to me and tells me to phone him. I phone him at home and ask him out for a drink. I can tell he doesn't want to, but he complies. As a joke I put his details into Ada's Engine to see what will happen. But Ada herself said that the Analytical Engine, as powerful as it might seem, could never generate new truths. It tells me what I already know from a different angle.

***

It didn't go well with Azad. I started to explain my theory of holistic data management, but he was uninterested. I was wearing my red shoes and red underwear, but they didn't make any difference. When holism didn't attract him, I switched to discussion of Ada Lovelace's Analytic Engine. He wasn't interested in the first woman in computer science, the first person to understand the potential for software before anybody else. He kept up a frowned look, which marred his otherwise beautiful features. When I mentioned she was Byron's daughter he showed more interest and we talked literature, but I couldn't get him interested in Virginia Woolf either. He thought it was funny my parents had named me after a character in one of her novels. I said I didn't find it very funny, and in order to shut him up I told him my father had hung himself and Virginia Woolf drowned herself. And anyway, I continued, Clarissa was also the name of a novel in which a woman gets raped by somebody called Lovelace and dies. It was difficult to get the conversation back on a more friendly tack after that and he got a text and said he had to go. It was a pre-arranged get-out, I'm sure, from Chloe. It was pure coincidence Ada ended up marrying somebody called Lovelace since he had nothing to do with Richardson's Clarissa. It's highly implausible that Chloe would meet Mark One at Ground Zero. That's one of the problems I'm working on with the Engine, how to cope with the possibility of coincidence. The improbable is a feature of the probable though, says Aristotle.

***

Mark One has just got back from New York. I was in bed. He showered and got in and then he was all over me. The jet-lag doesn't kick in until later so he thinks he can just come back and paw me. I told him it was too soon, not nice to be treated like that, to get some sleep, and we could make up and catch up later that day or in the evening. He was over-tired and I made some allowances, and when he finally got to sleep he muttered phrases from our times together, the good times and the bad ones, in sickness and in health. Everything, everything, even going out with Azad to make something, everything is nothing. Nothing can come of nothing. If I have to describe the feeling to you it is a vast chasm in my chest and misery in my head, and nothing but.

It's not depression. My dad had that.

The number 0 is not positive or negative. It is Rational and Real and Even. 0. If one set does not have any apples, the one has 0 apples.

The truth value is false, = 0.

The noose formed a 0 around my father's neck.

Antidepressants may increase the risk of suicide. My father took antidepressants, the older type. My father committed suicide. Nobody knows how antidepressants work. Nobody can measure the level of serotonin in the brain.

I wake Mark One up for a fuck, and picture Azad to make sure I come. When Mark goes back to sleep I increment the fuck column by 1 in the Engine. It reads 1,872.

I click on the Help icon. The Engine returns a null value.

***

Start Dream 316.
Nothing.
End of Dream 316.

***

The first middle manager I meet has a bald head and a beard. He's insisted somebody from Human Resources sits in. Nobody has told me this would happen. My job is to capture information and treat it holistically. What could be the problem? I can defer the meeting and ask Azad and Chloe, or go ahead with the meeting as if it makes no difference. Do I need to be this man's friend? I ask them why the meeting is set up like this. I don't know who I should be addressing, Tony and his real ale pullover, or Libby, tight skirt and the smile before oblivion. They tell me it's company policy, the Union, HR and the Corporation working together. Fine, I say. I ask my questions. Tony starts to patronise me, suggests he knows more about working processes than I'll understand in a lifetime of Sundays, whatever that may mean. I keep pulling him back to the questions in hand, trying to itemise the kinds of tasks his workforce do and the time required, and the level of person who can do each task. He asks about the task he's involved in now, the task of answering questions. This is not bean-counting I say. That's what you think, he says. Libby doesn't have an opinion, she's just there to observe, not facilitate. I note down the possibility of making answering questions a task. He

101

smiles. I see why he's not got further than he has, trapped as he is in a limited consciousness. Yes, I say, it is possible for me to gather in all the information and show the way forward. He'll be retired by then, he says.

I wonder to myself if there will be much more hostility. He thinks it's a staff-slashing exercise. Like Libby, I can't comment. He repeats that he'll be retiring soon, turns to Libby, nods, and tells her his wife died last year. The smile goes and she says she's sorry. I grind my teeth.

***

Mark One needs to talk when I get back.

'Shoot', I say.

'Look Clar, in New York . . .'

He doesn't tell me anything I didn't already know. It's not information. We agree to go our separate ways. Nobody will be hurt now the children have left home. He goes up to the attic and takes one of the girl's rooms until he can find somewhere else to live, without me. I retreat into the Engine, put in the necessary data about our relationship. The Field of Feelings returns a null value.

It brings back my father's suicide. My mother found him, hanging from ladders hanging from brackets in the centre of the ceiling that he'd fixed up years before. I phone mother. She's the motherth mother. This is the zeroth emotion.

***

Start Reality. 507.

I dream of the root of minus one, symbol i.

i.

I see now it's i. $i^2 = -1$.

Me times me = minus one.

I times I. Negative.

i is an imaginary number.

End Reality 507.

***

The Enchantress of Numbers

I was born Ada Augusta Byron in 1815.

My father died when I was 9.

He was Lord Byron. He died in 1824.

They were worried about family insanity, and taught me maths to stop me going mad. I caught measles, and was crippled and confined to bed and the number of children I had was an odd number, 3.

***

The problem with the Analytical Engine is precisely that it has no recourse to narrative disclosure, it cannot cognise the world as discourse, it cannot understand stories. *i* know this. *i* tried to get him to remember how we met and the good things that had happened since but Mark One did not understand. *i* asked him to tell me the story of us when he told me he was leaving. *i* put the story into the Engine. It returned null. *i* have now made the root of minus one a value where previously we had zero. Like the Mayans *i* have carved a symbol to represent the root of minus one. It is the image of *i*, my self. Anybody can do it, make an image of themselves to stand in for *i*.

***

i had my meeting with the first of the senior managers. He was more arrogant than the last until *i* pointed out the problems his company had and the money they were haemorrhaging. He went pale when *i* said that. 'Haemorrhaging' *i* repeated. *i* told him if they didn't stop that unwanted flow, they would haemorrhage senior staff, it was the only thing that would make sense. *i* suggested he visualise money as blood seeping out through the fistulas of his corporate creation. Now count down from tenth to first, *i* ordered. He did it. And then . . .? *i* prompted. Nothing, he said? Not quite, *i* corrected, it's 'zeroth'. Describe the zeroth. The new woman from Human Resources wanted to stop the conversation because she felt sick at zeroth, but he wanted to go on, because he was starting to see the whole picture. *i* told him he was thinking holistically now. Carry on counting down *i* said. He understood. He raced passed nothing to minus one. What's the square root of four? Two, he said. What's the square root of one, *i* asked. One he said. What's the square root of minus one? He didn't know, so *i* filled him in.

We got down to itemising the tasks he set his particular staff and the time each task attracted. Even with just two interviews the patterns were starting to emerge. *i* grind my teeth, dream of green leaves and yellow flowers, the empty note sounding *i*.

Joan Miró

The girl on the scrub ground took the dog off the lead where Abelard could just see. The dog retrieved balls and lost interest, bounding up the steps. Too much trouble to go out when he didn't like dogs. 'Almond. Almond'. The girl fetched Almond. '¡Ola!' she shouted to Abelard. He shooed her and Almond away.

***

'I am 50'.

Esperança snorted. 'Are you a baby? Nearly 51. Stay with the job this time'.

'I will. But not the double shift, it's too much. I'm 50. Look at that!'

On the screen a Russian ice-hockey team died. Esperança snorted. 'Don't change the subject. Stay with the job'.

'Yes, but not the double shift. Why are dogs called "Almond"?'

'Why not?

'Pah'.

***

'Can I speak to Ivan?'

'Ivan?'

'Yes, "Ivan". He gave me the job'.

'When?'

'Two weeks ago'.

'Which job?'

'What does it matter? I just need to speak to Ivan. Can I come up?'

'No. Try phoning'.

'But . . .'

***

The girl was on the ground with the dog retrieving balls. Abelard walked past and she shouted her greeting after him which he chose not to hear. He was taking over from Piet, who stood up.

'¿Did you see the building on the bottom of the left side?' asked Abelard. It looks like somebody started a fire, ¿heh?' Piet vacated his seat saying nothing and picked up his bag. It didn't look like he'd been reading anything, just staring out at the dog shit. When Abelard repeated his observation about the fire Piet shrugged and smiled. Abelard thought Piet was about half his age. When the dog came in Piet made a fuss and after he heard the girl shout 'Almond' he called it Almond cheerfully in his accent. It wasn't possible to shoo the girl and dog away when Piet was making friends of them. The girl introduced herself to Piet as Maria. Piet repeated 'Maria' and 'Almond'. Piet shouldn't be encouraging intruders, Ivan wouldn't like it. At mention of the name 'Ivan' Piet smiled and repeated it, 'Ivan'. When Piet went Maria greeted Abelard as if they were meeting for the first time, in a very simple manner, which made Abelard consider her in a new light. He shooed her away.

***

The boy with the deep voice came over with the beers.

'I'm tired', said Abelard to Enrique. 'I'm doing it to get Esperança off my back. I want to get out of the double shift but I can't find Ivan'.

'¿Who's Ivan?'

'¿What does it matter? I don't want to double-shift. That's all'.

'You never work, Abelard. Esperança has carried you all these years. She saved you from the curse of the vine. ¡A security guard! ¿Guarding what? ¿What job is that for a grown man who should be a scholar?'

106

'An empty apartment block. They will knock it down soon, and I will be out of a job, but I can't find Ivan to get out of the double shift'.

'¡Let's find Ivan!' Enrique disengaged to admire the old newspaper clippings about *Les Quatres Gats*. 'Picasso and Miró drank here', he burst out, 'a hundred years ago to this day. ¿Marvellous, eh?'

'¿Is that why you dragged me across the city to this shitty bar?'

'Better than Plaça del Centre'.

'¿You're not going to lecture me about art, are you? Let me tell you of the stories which haunt our empty buildings'.

***

Esperança, dyed reddish-black hair drawn back tight into a plait at the back. Glasses which are black with white frame sides and black leopard spots, long dangling earrings
white muslin dress dropping down to the ankles
flip flops with diamante toe-straps
wedding ring
wooden bangle on the right wrist
brown bra strap showing under the white dress straps
talks with her hands
has a dismissive gesture where she flicks her hand
a large silk scarf with ferocious swirls of violet, teal and taupe covers over her shoulders and the best part of her upper torso
inside her head knowledge of fifteen different languages to speak to hotel guests, to add gravitas

***

When Abelard and Esperança first met Abelard was one year into a biology degree, taken because he was interested in natural history, but couldn't settle to studying. When Esperança first met him she had liked this about him, thought he might be a famous scholar like his namesake. But, the curse of the vine.

***

What difference does it make to the dragonfly to know its Latin name? '¡The dragonfly knows it is Catalan!' Abelard would quip, with diminishing returns.

***

Esperança often wondered what her life would have been like if she had accepted Enrique's offer. But she loved Abelard. To this day she wondered, more and more about that other life with Enrique. His life as a book illustrator had been chequered. When digital software emerged for graphics he proved surprisingly adept as he despised it. But by then the spell of modernista was gone, had no effect on him, and nothing could replace it.

***

Abelard's studiousness had been the attraction, not the object of his study. After one of their arguments he went out drinking and she threw away his books and when he came back and she told him what she'd done, flicking her hand to swat his silence, snorting for the first time, she saw the light go out of his eyes. It was the start of the rest of their life together. Esperança wanted to say sorry later that day, instead found herself saying 'don't do that thing with your mouth, it's really annoying'. Over the next few weeks she tried to win him back with food, sex, and by replacing the books, but nothing could bring back the pantheistic Abelard. When she went to Enrique for help, he could only talk art to her, advised her to seek solace in the Blue Period, because, she realised, he had not forgiven her for choosing Abelard. When she tried to bring Enrique back through looking at the paintings, she only enjoyed the early realist depictions, representations before the start of the new century, where science and charity were recognisable human figures in Picasso's first success. This was life. But what was her life now? Blue, but not like those monochromes, which were a forced melancholy only. She was middle-aged, soon to be old, only her scarves had colour. One time Enrique explained why statues had to have no colour, it was all to do with form. Esperança told him it was stupid, waved her hand more vigorously than usual, and when she learned about the startling child reds, yellows and blues of 'Lovers Playing with Almond Blossom' she went and confronted him immediately. '¿What do you say to that?' Enrique smiled. It was 1980. He was losing his faith in the modernista, the sparse symbolism of Miró's stars, moons, suns and breasts in repetitive variation.

Enrique's sudden disregard for Miró pushed Esperança to seek him out. Miró's marks on paper became more real the more Abelard withdrew to his croney-filled existence and the curse of the vine. For twenty-five years she poured over what pictures she could find, visited the gallery when it opened after Miró's death, lost herself in the realer sensations of Miró, as if to replace Abelard's loss of faith in nature with her own faith in Miró, as if to replace the loss of Abelard with the presence of Miró. The symbols spoke only to her. The stars, here, just like that, filled Esperança.

***

Enrique goes to the empty apartment block – Ivan is there, he has sacked Abelard; Enrique thinks of all the stories that once happened of metaphysical necessity in the apartments; 'all the joys riddled with cancer' he thinks; he sees the girl throwing a ball for the dog to retrieve, and she has a parrot on her shoulder.

Esperança looks up at the sculpture in Park Joan Miró, lets its magnitude, unity, form and structure fill her.

Abelard has his back to the Familia Sagrada, watches the blue and red dragon flies on the pond opposite the disgusting building (he has been drinking); he will at last become an anarchist like his father, like those who destroyed Gaudi's drawings in the 20s, he will be life like dragonflies mating in mid-air not architecture, he will be like Abelard.

The Memory Clinic

Having been given the doubtful honour of putting Johannes Boanerges' literary estate in order I appear to have achieved very little, and may thus give the impression that perhaps I am not quite the friend I should be. My initial flush of success in laying out the key themes of his life – humanity and its obverse, genocide; animals; the removal of nation states and the pressing necessity for global benign dictatorships (I can't remember if I said that last one, but it's true, nor if I mentioned his interest in the early Nineteenth Century Russian short story writer and philosopher, Vladimir Odeovsky, also the inventor of the idea of social media, which I should have done); nothingness – was given a wobble when I discovered an unpublished essay of his entitled 'The Phenomenology of Shit'. He never spoke of it. But look, I was his closest friend, Victor(ia) notwithstanding. And through everything, despite the burden of sole responsibility for a legacy which may already have had its day – for others to judge – I have been thinking that what I admired most was his unfailing commitment. The cynical wag will say 'yes, his unfailing commitment to many, many things' and it is true that he had a large number of enthusiasms, too many to devote all his time to. But, if I could put myself forward for just this once, after which I will remove myself from the picture, the ability to commit to a cause is not something that characterises me. But Johannes, God bless, boy could he commit. Odeovsky had the idea houses could be connected by magnetic telegraphs to circulate our daily affairs. JB passed on to me Odeovsky's short story 'Two Days in the Life of the Terrestial Globe'. JB talked of initial causes.

I'm in the works cafeteria with V and hiser little shit, a man whose baldness acts as a statement of shiny intent. There are rings attached to the edges of both his ears, picking up signals from around the doomed terrestrial globe no doubt to pass into his tiny black eyes, onto thin lips which form the slit of a mouth. A skin-tight red t-shirt shows the contours of his stockiness and his fat belly. Every now and then he is talking to one of the women at the tills and making jokes with them and at other times he is taking an abandoned meal tray to the waste conveyor belt for processing. Is he working here or not? V, dressed in black Greek widow's weeds, is urging him to tell me about his charity work and looking at himer smiling and he is going all shy and wheeling his terrestrial globe in my direction and the same smile looking sinister when turning on me. He is lowering his eyes now in mock shyness which V is taking for the modesty of the charity worker. 'What are you doing?' he is asking and I am saying that I am trying to writing my own work at the same time as I am pulling together my good friend Johannes Boanerges' literary estate. 'What are *you* doing *for the world?*' he is clarifying for me and V is nodding like a noodle and he is holding his gaze. I am looking down and glimpsing his bare feet in sandals. How is it being that they are loving him and he is being repulsive for me alone?

V is declaring 'He is helping everybody, all the time! He is being committed! All the time, committing! All the time' and V's eyes are glistening. I am saying how odd it is that I am thinking of commitment and Johannes, how Johan was being there with the French students in sixty eight, with feminists in the seventies (penance for his alleged bigamy which was alleged in America in '66 allegedly?). If he were alive now he would be occupying the centres of global capitalism (keeping to himself the desire for benign dictatorships I am adding parenthetically in my head unkindly I am not being able to help it).

The little shit is smiling pointedly asking '*who* did he help? *how* did he help?', he really is being a shit, and V is smiling waiting for something from me, thinking that the little shit is asking a nice, fair question. '*He was helping humanity*' I am saying with greater emphasis and he is making me look down now at both of his bare feet which for some reason are coming out from under the table. Jesus sandals.

'Who are the humanity people?' V is asking.

'Everybody. You, me, little shits, everybody. Johannes loved them all, and was committed to loving them all'.

'How was he helping them?'

'He was protesting and writing books [you creeping Jesus]. He was signing up to Amnesty International and to campaigns for freeing political prisoners.

111

He was fighting against the death penalty [even though he sometimes felt it was justified]. Fighting! Johannes was a fighting man. He was being in prison, five times. I was forgetting this. I am writing it down now so I am not forgetting. Everything is always happening every now time'. I am taking out my pen and notepad and I am writing it down that Johannes was being in prison five times for his commitments and I am being buggered if I can remember all the five times he was being in prison so perhaps the little shit is riling me into exaggerating. 'In Paris, Sudan, Kenya, Britain, and . . .' Thinking thinking thinking.

The little shit's shiny globe is giving me a migraine and I am understanding migraines as a scrambling of everything, stopping me seeing everything. They are getting worse. I am getting old, the migraine whiteness at the edge of sight starting to encroach on the whole of my vision. 'I am having a migraine attack. Please be excusing me. Your Jesus, sandals, they are searing [into?] my brain, they are revolting, they . . .' I am moving to be getting up, puzzling over the fifth prison instance, trying to ignore the unignorable pain in my head, worrying about falling over, hating V and hiser little side-kick. V gently seats me in my distress and I am feeling too weak to resist. 'Migraine' I am muttering.

'Close your eyes' he is saying. 'Be mindful'. His voice is changing, is changed, is working its way into my block of head, insinuating its way into it. 'Be mindful' he soothes, 'of the pain, move with it, be its friend, hold it in your hands, gently now, gently, it is to be cherished, help it on its way back to where it came, move it out of your head, you are floating in outer space, it is moving out of your head, let it go, let it fly away from you, it is flying to the sun where it will burn and you will be well again after suffering. You will be well [falling cadence] you will be well'.

It wasn't working at all except I was grateful to him for taking care of me who detested him. The anxiety over the fifth prison wouldn't go away. Why wasn't I remembering? The migraines weren't helping memory and nor were they were hindering memory. The migraines were memory-neutral. 'The fifth prison' I am muttering over and over again, 'the fifth prison'. The little shit, for it was still he, continued to pour soothing words and images into me, with the premise and promise that I could disperse the pain in my head by easing it into the universe. I started to worry that if this worked, the whole universe would be the repository of everybody's pain, the whole universe would be a migraine that had the magnitude of the universe, and we, the human race would be free from suffering, dwelling in the universe of suffering yet without suffering ourselves, outside of all suffering, immune. The universe would suffer whereas we would not. 'The fifth prison' I am continuing to mutter, with the pain in my head worse than ever. Opening my eyes he is smiling and asking me 'better?' and V is willing me to say 'better' and for all I am not standing these people I am saying 'better' so that I am like them and he takes the opportunity to start talking about his charity work, in a way which even I must confess does not appear as self-aggrandising as it might. The little shit. V is heading off for more drinks for us, just water for me.

'I am building a guillotine' he says, when V is gone, 'for charity. You mustn't tell anyone, it is a secret. Yes?'

'Which charity?' could possibly want you to build a guillotine?

'The fifth prison' and he is laughing.

'That's the name of the charity?'

'The fifth prison! A guillotine for the fifth prison! Tell nobody. You and me', and he gives me the warning look.

As soon as V returns with my water and his latte, the conversation returns to normal. I haven't really ranted about 'the fifth prison', have I? He hasn't really talked about constructing a guillotine for charity, has he? There isn't really a charity called 'the fifth prison' is there? My ability to ask good questions is still in reasonable shape if nothing else. I was pretty out of it, still am, with the migraine. What people don't understand is that migraines last for hours. Even when they're fading, it feels like you have a headache 'scar', like the source of the pain is gone, yet the pain feels just as bad, it's just that there's nothing behind it *making* the pain. *There is nothingness and there is pain — simultaneously. The pain makes you feel the nothingness behind it.*

'I'm sorry if I said anything out of turn. My head was hell'. They both understood, but I can't remember what I've said out loud, what I've hallucinated, and what I've thought. 'There really is no fifth prison'. They both nod, slightly puzzled. 'There really isn't. I don't remember how many there were, but Johannes definitely was in prison a number of times. He never backed down from his causes, even the idiotic ones. Unless it was Margaret Thatcher put him there, in the fifth prison'. The migraine has removed the module in my head marked 'ratiocination'.

***

Cognitive enhancement. I've taken the pill and come to the meeting with the express purpose of remembering Johannes's commitment, trying to think thematically about his life, not chronologically. I would like to organise his collected works thematically, not chronologically. I did explain to Christina that I didn't have dementia or anything, this really was to find out about general memory improvement, I'm not forgetful myself, I just need to remember better. The rest of the bunch were frail in the main, struggling to cling on to the bowels of reality. We began with remembering what we had for breakfast. Some of them couldn't even remember that. I was in the wrong place. 'Scrambled eggs on toast'. There were two Iraq wars, weren't there? Johannes supported them both. 'Just wars' he would say. One of his best friends was an Iraqi Kurd, Sana, and she wanted Saddam Hussein killed. 'Then let's kill him' said Johannes, 'this monster cannot live. I have the PM's ear'. She was very pleased with the Americans and the British, and so was Johannes. He could not understand, for himself and for Sana, why people would not want Saddam dead. It made no sense to him when people approved of going into Kosovo but not Iraq. He committed to Sana's cause.

'Thank you, Narr', thanks Christina, 'your memory is working very well!'

'I am writing a book about Johannes Boanerges', I continue, 'my good friend and a great philosopher, novelist and poet. Well, maybe not a great poet, prose was his forte. It is a big responsibility, and I worry that I can't accurately remember how things were'. Nobody has heard of him, not a single one. I quickly aggregate the number of earth years that have been lived in the room. Close to a thousand years, and not one memory of Johannes. What is life, then, if nobody remembers the great Johannes Boanerges? 'Johannes Boanerges, the great and famous philosopher. Lived to be 104. His work has improved our lives'.

'Thank you again, Narr. We need to move on to Harriet. Harriet, what did you have for breakfast?'

This is a rather large circle of us sat remembering, twelve of us, each with a head full of holes. It's going to be twenty or thirty minutes before we get back to me. They are trying to remember food from this morning. I am trying to remember the texture of our lives from twenty, thirty, forty, fifty (really?) years ago. Sana was gloomy and committed to a Kurdish homeland. Why shouldn't we kill Hussein? He was killing her people. And the weight of opinion was on

114

Sana's side before the war, and then it started to fall away. An intellectual was not allowed to say that war was good. Johannes had no academic allegiance. He spoke the truth to power! War is good (sometimes)! I say all this.

'Thank you, Narr. We do need to move on. Harriet, what did you have for breakfast?'

I fume and sulk. Sulky fuming. After Harriet, Henry, our youngest nonagenarian – who looks better than me: bone structure, it never deteriorates – opens up the mysterious neurological portals. Why wasn't I blessed with bone structure? Why, why?

'I remember him . . . followed him after the war in the papers. Jonas, yes, Jonas'.

'Jonas?'

'Your pal, Jonas'.

'My friend the great philosopher's name is *Johannes*'.

'Yeah, I know, but we called him Jonas. He interviewed me and some of the other conchies. Said that the world would disappear into the sun, or something like that, thanks to the Nazis. A bit daft like. Had a funny accent. They wanted to lock him up cuz they thought he were a Nazi. Always wanting to get me to the pub. I don't drink which is why I'm so old. There were a petition from famous writers like the Sunday man poet to keep him out'a prison. What were 'is name?'

'Tom?'

'Charlie?'

'Hermann? No, not Hermann, he *were* a Kraut, they sent him to a POW camp'.

'No, Hermann were another conchie. He ended up in Winson Green'.

I look imploringly at Christina to arrest this nonsense. 'I think we are upsetting Narr'.

'Sorry Narr'.

(Henry) 'Broomhill. That's where we were. He wrote a poem about it. Not Jonas, the poet, wrote it. The Institute were up at Broomhill where the students are. It's what I remember, anyhow. Your pal Jonas visited us conchies'.

'Why would *Johannes*, Henry, talk to you conchies? What is a conchie?'

'"Conscientious objector". He said he were interested in studying the . . .'

(Interruption from Anne) 'You were a conchie? *You were a conchie?!* My husband died fighting while you were swanning it up in Broomhill? Henry, I never had you down for a coward, never. I'm not sure I can be in the same room now I know this'. She furiously backs the wheelchair out of the circle and speeds off at an angry 6.7 mph, breaking the clearly visible speed limit for the room ('no faster than 5 mph, please', Sheffield Hospitals Institute Trust) crashing into the wall. The other helper clears up the mess and takes Anne out, confused and ranting. The memories are coming back to the group thick and fast now. Christina starts to explain how it is often our formative years which are the ones we remember most, and many of the . . .

'Henry, I don't think your Jonas is my Johannes' I insist, 'he never mentioned anything to me about interviewing conscientious objectors, and I was his best friend for forty years, fifty if we include the ten years since his death when I have been collating his papers and thinking how best to present his genius to the world'.

'Please yourself. He was a commie. *I* was back then as well, of course, changed after the war. We argued about the war. He said it was a just war, killing Nazis. Said they weren't human. He were a Jew-boy, weren't he? Smart, but daft like. We all felt sorry for the Jews, really. Are you Jewish?' I show Henry the picture of JB I keep in my wallet – 1967, arm around Guy Debord, regulation Gitane gangling about the mouth (did JB smoke back then? I can't remember). 'Aye, that's him'.

'That's him' I nod to the room, one of the group now. Henry correctly identifies Johannes in the photograph: 'Yep, that's Jonas'.

'Johannes'.

'Jonas'.

'Why did you object? And what were you objecting to? Killing Nazis?'

All this time Christina has been trying to interrupt and regain control of the group. It happens every session – once the memories come back it's a flood and the members start to form their own mini-memory groups of twos and threes. Christina's got some research going on about the cognitive enhancement drugs she's plying us with, which is why she's so keen on the sessions. We know some of us must be on placebos, but as far as it's possible to tell there's not much difference between any of us, we're as good and as bad as each other at the memory game. Christina shushes us. I'm all abuzz with this new information about Johannes. The man never ceases to amaze me, dead though he be. Interviews with conscientious objectors! Conchies! Whatever next!

Henry can't remember what he had for breakfast. Neither can I, or did I already say 'scrambled eggs on toast'? We have something else in common and agree to meet up later on.

On my way out of the room, Christina ushers me to one side and takes me into her confidence: 'Remember – old people tell stories' and chases after a couple of mobility scooters breaking the speed limit. I'm sure she means that old people tell tall tales, and for me to be wary of Henry. Or is she implying that *I* am embroidering? Does she consider me one of the old people? I'm not quite seventy yet, after all.

On my way out of the building I see the little shit at the far end of the corridor pushing a patient on a trolley, part of his charity work, according to V. He is a good man, no doubt, building a private guillotine. Was that fifth prison really during the poll tax, or was it another stint in Paris, 1968? Guy Debord filched JB's ideas, which is why they fell out. How committed was this Guy to revolution? Was JB? JB was never in tune with his times, not really. I admit he could be a faddist, but he continued to argue for just war until his death, so there was commitment there. The idea of 'a just war' is not fashionable now that it's been taken over by Jihadists, let's face it. JB's plan, I suspect, was first to replace all malignant tyrants with benignant tyrants and this would involve a just war. Then, replace all remaining democracies with 'benarchies' (*Benarchy*, his last book-length publication on politics, 1998; I will try to get this reprinted – this is one of Joho's most prescient commentaries. If not – then what? I hardly have to suspect the plan, it's what the whole of *Benarchy* is about). I'm sure all of these things will come together in the end, in spectacular fashion, and heaven will become earth, and earth heaven . . .

***

A sunny summer Sunday in Broomhill, home of the Sorby Research Institute as was. Henry explains how tough it was to be a conscientious objector. The environment is beautiful. Wide roads, trees everywhere, stately buildings set back from the road in their own grounds, modern additions carefully hidden. Henry can't remember if this is the actual building, so it will have to do. There are a couple of yellow O'Brien skips outside into which have been poured fractured spars and ash-plaster. A short man with a blazing globe of a head is dispensing with papers into the container, none other than V's little shit. 'You're following me about' he shouts as we go up the drive. 'Am I?' I shout back. The thought of confrontation makes me feel my age, although Henry at my side gives me a strange feeling of security. Johannes never backed down from anything, something he attributed to what he saw as a teenager and as a young man in his twenties without elaborating (another gap in our JB knowledge that will need to be filled somehow. Where will I find the time?). The universal porter proceeds to ignore me; I can smell the stink of his armpits even when he goes back inside for more rubbish. Henry and I are both in our jackets and ties, preserving standards. The temperature is pushing thirty-two degrees and Henry says it is important not to take off the jacket or tie. Imagine you are in combat, he says, in the Sudan or advancing on Aleppo (why these places?) and you have no choice. We mustn't drink any water either, and he laughs, a little insanely. 'Mallenby! Pure Mallenby!'

'Did you consent?', I ask, 'were you aware of what you were letting your-self in for?'

'We were helping medical science to benefit humanity'. He wears a smile for me and nods, sweating. I'm pretty thirsty and move under a nearby beech for shade. Henry follows me. I need to lose him so I can sneak a drink. 'You stay here', I say, 'let the state of the surrounding geography be the state of your mind', and I hug him and thump his back so that he understands my complete sincerity. Such nonsense confuses him and I move out of the shade towards the skip and its contents, discovering that amongst the papers being trashed are some that relate to the conchie experiments, mainly hate mail of one kind or another that we must imagine aren't deemed worthy of preserva-tion. On the one hand it is remarkably fortuitous that I should happen across documents relating to some unexplored period of Johannes's life, on the other hand somewhat ironic that the material affords me little in the way of usable

118

material. The little shit comes out of the building with more box files and chucks them in. To avoid eye-contact I turn away and shout to Henry stood under the beech tree (it's a copper beech, by the way, adding lustre to his gentlemanly status) that there is hate mail to him and his conchie friends from way back when. 'Shall I get some water?' I don't wait for an answer and ask the only person in the vicinity where the nearest place to get water is. He smiles and goes back in the building leaving me dazzled with the sunbeams that have bounced off his bonce. The sunblindness prevents me from being able to read the new batch of old documents. I'm so thirsty, I keep gulping, as if this will bring water into my mouth. 'Henry', I shout across, 'let's go inside and get some water from the toilets'. The one-time conscientious objector heroically stands his ground, refusing to take in water. If only I had his fortitude! Perhaps the stately copper beech affords him an inner strength.

The little shit bars my path into the house, saying it's a demolition site. 'Where's your hard hat?', I ask. He ignores me, turns around and goes back in. Now, shall I follow him? There's a bare foyer and an impressive staircase and he disappears into a space beyond the stairs. I move in, thirst uppermost in my mind, Henry second, Johannes third, the project fourth, a short story about the end of the world fifth, a mental image of Henry under the copper beech imbibing the qualities of the landscaping sixth, and seventh an uneasiness about that very image. The stench of unwashed armpits precedes the return of the short stocky man. He has removed his trademark tight red t-shirt. Both his nipples are pierced and there is a tattoo 'CHARITY' above his left breast. 'I'm desperate for a drink', I beg. This is suburban hell – no sign of shops, no sign of sustenance, some kind of civilised social engineering experiment gone wrong, too much heat and too little Henry. 'Please, please, I need a drink. I'm an old man, and so is the man out there. Please, I'm sweltering in this heat. It's so hot'.

'Go home. Leave my friend alone'.

'Friend? Which one? Her? Him? Himer?'

'You know. V(mumble) Now go'.

'I have permission to be here'. I gulp. How many more times can I check my mouth for moisture before collapsing? Why didn't we bring our own water? Henry is depending on me I'm sure to bring out the water. I move to the doorway out the foyer to see Henry still stood there, not even leaning on the tree, not asking for anything, at home with peace in a world at war with itself. 'For the sake of that man there', I plead, pointing, 'water!' There is difficulty adjusting my eyes when he turns away into the gloom of the building. It looks like his back has a tattoo of a guillotine with my head on the block. I turn back to Henry, the sun high in the sky, getting closer every minute, burning up the blue, hammering down on the people of the earth. The suffering has not dissipated, it has coalesced in me, Henry falls to the ground and the little shit emerges with a bottle of water, pushes past me, and tends to my fallen comrade. I try to keep up with him, and when I eventually get there he is knelt behind him, holding him gently, offering sips from the translucent blue plastic bottle, Henry, thin as a rake, starved and dessicate, dying under the midday sun. Desperate, I wrestle with both of them for the bottle – 'Just one mouthful, one mouthful, don't deny me! I'm not strong enough to go on without water!' I am pushed back to the ground, hated. If Henry doesn't need the water, why can't I have it? I'm an old man. He is trying to kill me for no good reason. Seeing that there is no profit in staying in the environment of a copper beech tree, a little shit and a recently expired conscientious objector, surrounded by lawns and stone walls and manicured lawns and the absence of retailers, being beaten down upon by the murderous suburban Sunday sun, I creep back to the skip, hoping that there at least may be something for the JB record. Somebody calls for an ambulance.

***

I'm itching itching itching on my wrists and groin and throw back the sheet to start scratching below when I see that I am naked and sitting next to the bed are V and the little shit. On the other side are some flowers on a bedside table, a copy of *Benarchies* and a box folder marked 'Kenneth Mallenby'. I can barely take all of this in so maddened am I by the creepy-crawly skin. V pulls the bedsheet up to the top of my hips. It's funny that I have never become habituated to the site of my grey pubic hair, a source of deep shame.

The Little Shit looks about him and then pulls out a small unmarked jar with a lotion. 'Here, from the Institute', he whispers. His voice is soft, know-ledgeable, caring, and I understand what V sees in him. I'm so beside myself with the itch in my groin and the inside of my wrists that I simply cede all control to him and he takes it upon himself to smother the affected areas. There is a gradual easing off of the irritation and he says that the cream should last a couple of hours. His globe appears as shiny as ever in the white of the hospital and another sunny day in a south-facing room. V smiles. If everything wasn't so wrong I would count my blessings.

'Terry says you've got scabies'.

'You picked it up the other day'.

'At the one-time Sorby Institute?'

'Maybe, I don't know about the Institute, do I?'. He does know though because I can see it in his eyes and if I can get V out of the way I will ask him.

'What have they done with Henry, the man I was with?'

'He's fine, just needed rehydrating, didn't he? Insisted he shouldn't take water, talking about an experiment. The paras told him the war was over and he said o.k. He sure is one tough nut'.

I was about to say 'for a conchie' and thought better of it. V left for tests on her leg – she hadn't come to see me specially but had just been passing through. The eye at the back of her knee was clouding over and the consultant was caught between treating it conventionally and giving it a new name.

I asked Terry if he would leave me the lotion.

'I can't do that, it's not approved, is it? You caught the scabies off Henry's wartime suit, I'll be bound. Oh, I know all about the Institute and Mellanby. This is Mellanby's Lotion, works a treat, much better than modern-day stuff, glorified calamine. No, I couldn't leave it with you, the fruits of unethical medicine'.

'It would be the charitable thing, Terry'.

'Charity when it suits you, eh? Just remember, I'm building that guillotine. More lotion? Get yourself discharged and meet me at my house. Ask V for the address. See ya'.

'Show me your back'.

Terry smiled, turned his back on me, lifted the t-shirt, showed me the guillotine tattoo. There were no features for the face of the man operating the machine and no features for the man waiting for the angled blade of death. I couldn't help myself.

'You're not really building a guillotine, are you? Terry?'
'It's an act of charity, believe me pal'.

***

Benarchy
Manifesto

Now is the time, I sing, for a world of Benarchy
Now is the time, I sing, for the fully human
State, government, society, duty, freedom, I sing
The annihilation of State, government, society, duty, freedom, I sing
Prosperity, I sing
Health, I sing
The Benarchist, I sing
The human, we sing

Since time immemorial, there are goats and sheep, lions and lambs: this,
    we cannot change
Since time immemorial, there are wars: this, we cannot change
Since time immemorial, we have loved, we have hated: this, we cannot
    change
The fully human is all these things: goat, sheep, lion, lamb, murderer,
    companion
Benarchy embraces the fully human

Desire is all

This, our suffering globe, hurtles into the belly of the sun
We, the creature that knows suffering, hurtles into the belly of pain

The nation state is at an end
The national state is at an end
Difference is universal and transhistorical

Some understand more than others, this we understand
There is one who understands more than all the others
This, we understand is the Benarchist.

The Benarchist will govern without government
The Benarchist will be exactly human: the pig speaketh not
The Benarchist means well: warning, oregano is not basil
The Benarchist ensures the human is the good
The Benarchist cannot change the human
The Benarchist, through force, through reason, through love, will ensure
    the human

I was about to throw down the book. It was not how I had remembered it at all. Had I moved on from such ineffective JB self-indulgence? Was I leaving JB behind? I skimmed through the rest of the slim volume, alighting on passages which actually seemed quite reasonable and well argued: in the first half, 'Is the State an Abstraction?', 'Is there such a thing as neutral government?'; in the second half the operation of Benarchy, controlled by Johannes's favoured 'strong man'. A nurse came in and checked the chart at the bottom of the bed. We looked at each other. She didn't even smile, continued her tour of the ward. What were the others in for? I was about to throw down the book first for making no sense and now for being bland. The second half though, this Benarchy, this Benarchist. The Benarchist was both a person in the Benarchy and the leader of the Benarchists. At first JB talks exactly as if the Benarchist is the strong man, but then it resolves itself: we are all Benarchists, sheep and goats, at war and loving. Had JB finally ditched his strong man theory? 'Benarchy': well-meaning and without visible government. Each person a fusion of all elements that could make the human. Each person, fully human. This was wishful thinking, not theory, not revolution.

But then, then, he does tackle the beasts of contemporary political and economic theory: *neo-liberalism, globalisation, capitalism*. And for each one he demonstrates wrong-headedness, how each view, how each description, how each philosophy, must fail because it has not grasped what it is to be human. He mentions and discards 'global warming' and 'the environment'. *Mellanby*, he says, *turned away from the human to the environment. This turning away is a turn a back on.* And that's all. It occurred to me that the person who would best fit JB's ideal Benarchist would be Napoleon. And that should be the end of it. There is a disconnected subsection on 'Atrocity and Cruelty', but these certainly belong somewhere else. Why are certain acts deemed 'atrocities'? This leads him up a blind alley. Rather, it leads him in the same direction as some of the other works around genocide and he returns to the Benarchist. Pah! Napoleon! Pah!

But he is right to ask: why is democracy weak? Why is democracy *not the answer*? 'Demockery' he calls it in the book, one of his many playful neologisms.

A girl came in and complained her head had fallen off. What, really, was the complaint? I couldn't remember. I was asleep now and woke up at Terry's. Somehow he had acquired a large house in Broomhill, familiar looking, and V had dropped me there and wouldn't come in, shehe had another hospital appointment. Scattered around the guillotine were documents intended for the skip. In some senseless act, Terry had rescued them. The first I picked up was Mellanby's letter to somebody called Hugh Clegg at the *British Medical Journal* asking if he could attend the Nuremberg Trials as their foreign correspondent, worried that human experimentation would be given a bad name by the Nazis, wanting to rescue all the human experimentation data. The guillotine was in the front room. He had removed the room above to give more space to the guillotine. 'Rather French?' I said. 'It's eight-foot high. You could make one six-foot high. This one's eight-foot'. 'It must have taken a long time to build'. 'Of course. Two years. I have a full-time job, and the charity work takes up a lot of time. The charity work comes first'.

The oddest thing was that it was in the front room, in broad daylight. That was really odd. Keeping it in a dungeon where the sun don't shine – that would be dingily acceptable.

'Is it fully functioning?'

'Yes. D'you want to see it?'

I didn't really want to see it working and went back to the hospital to see if the girl was all right. I took some of the papers with me. V came and went for more tests.

When I knew I was better I returned to Terry's house. He'd collected some of the papers into a pile. 'I don't read German', he said, so we got V in, who does (her talents continue to amaze; my hostility remains). The police called round and checked on the guillotine in a friendly manner, joking that there hadn't been any recent decapitations in the area so he wasn't under any kind of suspicion at all, other than that of 'general intention' which a court had yet to decide. Terry got them to sponsor him for a cycle ride to Bruges, money going to the children's hospice. I was getting used to the guillotine. Why couldn't I like him?

The documents related to Dachau from what V said and must have been documents that Mellanby brought back from the trials. Terry started to reveal that he knew quite a bit about Mellanby, and it explained why he'd been there hovering round the skip that day, looking for Mellanby-related materials. 'He never showed these to anybody, he couldn't have'.

'What is it?'

Even though Terry couldn't read German he worked out that they were test results from experiments. Mellanby always claimed he had these, Terry explained. V translated some of the tests, the high altitude, the malaria, the extreme cold, the bullet wounds. 'It could be that Mellanby thought better of the whole affair, cried off. No, it says he thinks we should use the results, it will be of benefit'.

Terry looked at me and V looked up from the papers, understanding perfectly. We were now in Mellanby's position. Should we make the papers available? Was it our decision? V had to get off to the clinic, to have that third eye looked at.

Outside the sun and here the light glinting into the darkest recesses of our lives; here the human on the planet, confusing, confused, special, burning itself up in the heat of a battle it had no equipment for. The sun moved closer, threatening to fire up the Dachau documents, to release the steel blade, to fuse myself, Terry, Johannes, Mellanby, the street, V, Harry into a single mash of fleshy transcendence. Terry's globe shone in charity, reflecting light, bringing light, offering light to the world. Inside of us the sun was flaring, live-giving, death-giving, earth-giving. Terry had come through fire somewhere in his life and committed himself. I was struggling to remember what my purpose was, blinded by the sun's unforgiving white light and the guillotine and the shine off Terry's burnished skin.

Portuguese Tungsten

A distant cousin gulped Carla's lager and pushed it back, 'American Music' tattooed in gothic between his pecs, with clefs bass and treble left and right of the stomach. Conversation between him and the girls continued upon the girls wasting themselves the night before. Two times the younger of the waiters sat down with the group and listened in before returning to the bar. All the shots were grappa based, too big to be shots, and there were two for each of the three teenagers. Carla, fleshy mother in shades, sat unconcerned when the distant cousin made tangential comments to her about his not buying the beers. At other tables on the decking a couple of families with young children sought burgers and chips in the cool, the adults pretending not to be disturbed by the oaths of Carla. The other waiter came to explain the shots were made in Portugal but they didn't take in the information and he went back to his station after tidying five tables. From here to the sea was about a hundred yards across a foot-hot light-brown sand and at this time of the afternoon the wind picked up to a speed that was just the wrong side of comfortable, made the awning flap too loudly, the sections of yellow and white-striped fabric not always able to block the sun overhead.

A man with a large red gut stepped onto the boards, greeted them in the same soft southern drawl, lowered himself next to Carla and ordered a lager, sure to lean back and survey his wife and children, watchful of the lad's influence on his family. His talk to nobody at all was of the places they'd been before reaching the Algarve: Barcelona, Madrid and Lisbon. The other conversation was stuck on drunkenness. The cousin said something and the father

126

picked up on it and asked 'What's my name?', 'Richard', 'What's a nickname for "Richard"?', 'Dick', 'I don't want to become a "Richardhead", you understand?'

Later the young ones flicked beer at each other and tipped some on the table so Richard shouted across

'If you're going to act like children I'm going to treat you like children. This is a nice restaurant. Somebody owns this restaurant, and he works hard for this restaurant. If you can't be polite you can get the fuck out of here. I'm serious'. The young people were chastened but he repeated himself word-for-word.

When the women and children at one of the tables left a man to finish his meal and pay the bill, a waitress offered him a glass of port on the house. Another woman turned up to join the Americans, and Richard introduced her as Croatian. She spoke Portuguese to the waiter in an elegant way, and soon after that interchange a Croatian partner joined so that the group was larger. He had flowing curly hair (the American boy's was short, and his face pock-marked), and laughed a lot without saying much. The boy said to the distant uncle 'you need to change your attitude old man'. I expected a fight.

II

On the way up to the old town the English girl was delighted by a little grey Scottie dog belonging to nobody that tip-toed in front of her. When she asked her mother if she could stroke it the answer was 'no'. Her brother was amused and showed her the poster for a bullfight in Albufeira the weekend, and told her what they did to bulls. Perhaps they could go to the bullfight and see them do it for real. At the top of the hill, still with the sun streaming into the resort, they encountered the central square, and the dog disappeared. Narrow streets went off into the older parts. In front of a house next to the neat civic park sat Hector, his front door open, his walking stick held to one side. Beneath his white shirt was the Walter P38 he'd used to thwart the German desire for Portuguese tungsten in the last World War. Hector saw the English girl puzzled by the dog's disappearance and shouted to her where it was (in the small enclosed park next to his house), but his old age and poor teeth and ill health and unfamiliar language gathered into a frightening picture for the siblings. Father did his best to be diplomatic, spoke no Portuguese, and the incident remained a breach in the European fabric.

Turning into the main drag the sun drove straight into their faces. Up and down the incline the thickening crowd shifted, looking for gifts to take home, or for food. It was too early for unaccompanied teens and twenty-somethings to come out to play in bars. People watched from restaurant terraces when a man laid out on a deep-red cloth mat wood carvings of giraffes and couples kissing, and a young tanned woman in bead necklaces next to him gradually opened out a trestle table. Everyone wondered what would be on the table. From a distance the only items she had were two small toolboxes and all the passers-by and all the people waiting for food or launching into their starters were transfixed, discoursing amongst themselves on what she could possibly put on the table, moving to her own casual rhythm, wandering off for five minutes at a time, leaving all her stock and capital to the vagaries of a public conscience. The English family looked on with the rest as the Americans passed underneath, pausing a little at the wooden figures before continuing down to the bottom where the street opened out into the harbour and where outside the restaurants whole fishes were grilled in full view.

Behind the English in the same restaurant was a group comprised of two Scottish families. They were set back from the front of the terrace and couldn't see the stalls, so instead they passed around their digital cameras and looked at the pictures from the day, quizzed the waiter on cataplana, settled for garlic bread starters and non-Portuguese mains, except the one man who had the king-prawn kebabs from a vertical metal skewer contraption. Across the road a retired English couple looked down on the stalls. The sun kept coming down from the cloudless sky. Hector shut his front door and started his constitutional, stick in hand, gun secured in its original leather holster beneath the shirt, its outline visible to the police.

The Americans came back up the hill and settled on the restaurant with the retired couple. They sat down on tables next to this couple and were joined by the Croatian couple, all talking loud enough to be heard on the facing restaurant terrace. The distant cousin continued to talk in his non-committal way to the girls, his top covered by a plain white t-shirt. The girls continued talking, reminding him of the times when they played together as kids, and

128

they looked at some of the old photos of them Carla sent round from her bag, and every time the photo ended up in the father's hands he would say 'I got it'.

An odd couple who had just got married stopped by the woman's stall. In close up the service on offer was to engrave names on sea shells for fifteen euros. That was why the girl had tool boxes. The couple, from quite different and unequal parts of the world, were cheerful and were going to take up the offer, and everybody involved kept smiling, including the man who had sold a giraffe.

Richard ordered grilled sardines with chips and salad. When the plate arrived he systematically severed the head from the fish, then the tail, and then ate the trunk, bones and all. When he got to the sixth and final fish a dark grey liquid oozed out from the severed head. Nobody else in the group noticed his recoil. What did the liquid represent? His first and only thought was a putrefaction of the fish's brain. The normally edible flesh tasted bitter, like the inedible meat closest to the head, and after three mouthfuls he moved on to the chips, hiding the uneaten fish in the debris from the others so as not to offend the chef or demonstrate his ignorance of what fresh sardines should be like.

Below, the Scottie dog ran through the crowd, followed by a mongrel the size of a greyhound, shaggy but thin. The new dog was totally insane, ignored the adults and went up to the children, barked at them and came close to biting them, going from one child to another as if it had a plan for all of the children in the resort, and made them cry. The Portuguese looked on, unconcerned. The younger children became hysterical, either after a visit from the dog, or in anticipation of its visit. The dog became bolder and ran in and out of the bars, shops and restaurants. But what would happen if this became a regular occurrence? Some of the Portuguese understood that the tourist economy would collapse, that the entire service industry would be finished. It wasn't fair, the dog wasn't their fault. Inside themselves they too started to panic. The American father was oblivious, concerned that having eaten some of the tainted meat he would become ill and die far from his home. People would say that in dying he shirked responsibility for his family, responsibility for his relatives, responsibility for his friends, and that it was his fault he died. The dog was nothing to him. All around people were seized with fear, not knowing what to do, in their hearts wishing the dog would vanish so they could be saved. When the dog bit a little boy, the dog had gone too far and something had to be done. The Americans looked out and down onto the events. The lad with 'American Music' and musical clefs tattooed under his white t-shirt mentioned about the dog, and Carla uttered a curse word.

After biting the little boy the dog left off attacking and stood barking and bearing its teeth in the clearing of its own making, tracing out circles in a systematic fashion. It was better than nothing, yet there was still the worry the dog was out of its mind or at its wit's end and would bite again. Hector sat down outside a bar, close to where the dog was, laid his stick against the wall, above which Brazil were playing Argentina in the Copa America, live. He unbuttoned his white shirt, unbuttoned his holster, pulled out the loaded pistol and fired two shots directly into the head of the dog. Hector beamed at everybody. He had saved the resort and the Portuguese economy, the dog's blood on the nearby tourists formed badges of honour they could be proud of. Richard yelled 'fucking animals' resolutely. Everybody looked at him and his table, and then back at the dog with half its face missing, bubbles of blood on the newly-cobbled street.

III

Initially there were some sun beds with towels on them at the far end of the pool. About four longstay English took it upon themselves to break the rule of not reserving beds and finally took occupancy. Most of the sunbeds were this end, and nobody had broken the rules. An American woman with three children had just come out from an early dip. They were all extremely polite and what they said could not be heard beyond their own circle. After drying they didn't stay to burn and cool.

The beds were gradually taken up by a majority of English, then some Dutch and a Swedish family. The heat built quickly and dampened any enthusiasm. A boy and girl spent some time jumping in the pool, then doing handstands underwater, got out and had ice-creams. The American boy and girls appeared in the pool, along with Carla. There was a beach ball, with green and white stripes, which they hit between themselves. Rules gradually crept in regarding how the ball had to be hit and kept out the water. Their energy was great, and somehow lifted the spirits of all those around the pool on sunbeds, all those who were invariably quiet and relaxed. People from the apartment balconies hanging over the pool looked down and smiled as they checked their drying swimsuits. The father with the big red gut came and dived in without testing the water, tried a couple of strokes, then joined the group. His Croatian friend came a little later. 'Hey, here's a rookie', and they taught him the rules of the game. The newcomers' energy added to the energy of the vibrant girls and the boy with 'American Music' and musical clefs tattooed on the front part of his body. Nobody else went in the pool when the Americans and the Croatian man were in there. The Croatian woman came and just stayed on the side, watching, like everybody else.

People went to the pool bar and got snacks and watched the Americans from that vantage point. Some left the apartment block to eat lunch in restaurants, joking that they hoped the Americans wouldn't be in the pool when they got back. But the Americans stayed in the pool, playing the same game, hitting the ball between themselves so that it didn't go into the water or onto the poolside.

The King of Ivy

In a relatively short space of time Dinky Taylor became the King of Ivy. It was his doing and his downfall, though it began simply enough.

He and Theresa had moved in together the year before, just before she gave birth to Grace. Dinky had been attracted to Theresa because of her name, which he thought Catholic. His affection for her grew from this shallow observation. For Theresa, Dinky had materialized at just the right time, as she drifted in and out of drugs and the Brighton scene. Dinky had cleaned himself up six months earlier and was able to show her the way ahead, otherwise, as she knew very well, she would backslide. They decided to move North where it was cheaper, colder, more honest, as they saw it. In the South, everybody was your friend, but the friendships were shallow, never took hold, everybody drifting in and out. One day, lazing on the pebbled beach, looking at the burnt-out pier they loved so much, the sun behind setting over the sea at Hove, Theresa six months pregnant, they pledged their love to each other and upped sticks.

A year on from when they first met, with Theresa confident in herself and as a mother, the power in the relationship shifted her way. Dinky may have had the strength to put bad habits behind him, but there were no good habits to cling to. When Theresa was still vulnerable, she had filled the vacuum, and even though there was Grace to keep them occupied, Theresa monopolised the child and Dinky couldn't find consistent work. He odd-jobbed, skilled in nothing, building sites, shifting rubbish. She knew she had to feed his ego, fill his time, make him feel useful, although as we will see, her hold on him changed throughout the year. And there was one genuine thing she hated about the house, which was the ivy on the wall.

Dinky had been attracted to the street because all the houses were covered in ivy, and this made it olde worlde and distinctive. The area had been created at the end of the nineteenth century, and the rows of terraces had an unappealing uniformity. The story of this street was part of the estate agent blurb. The Master Builder had planted a tub of ivy against the wall of his house at the top of the street at the top of the hill. Over the following century the ivy had gone from top to bottom so that the forty-seven houses on that side of the street were covered in what from a slight distance looked like a plush, dark green carpet.

But Theresa hated the ivy. She had kept quiet because she had been desperate to move. A previous boyfriend had tracked her down to Brighton (she came from St Austell) and he was a nasty specimen. He had once thrown boiling water at her, and her right leg remained scarred. In a hurry to get out of Brighton, and with the pledge of love boosting her sense of esteem, she had agreed to the ivied street in a South Yorkshire town. There was the confidence to get out of Brighton, but it was to take a year to get Dinky to tackle the ivy. When it came to it Theresa didn't beat about the bush and after a few months within that year she had told Dinky she hated the ivy and that it had to come off her house. Dinky knew he couldn't contradict her. The way she said it he knew it was a thing that had to be done some time.

At the beginning of the year in the new house, although Theresa knew in the future that Dinky would have to get the ivy off the house, she initially suppressed her hatred for the ivy. This was so that the birth of Grace would be a beautiful affair. The pregnancy had been trouble-free, and their mutual fear that poisons from their previous lifestyle choices might have lingered in their blood streams and dna and be passed on to the foetus appeared to be unfounded. Pleased by the baby's steady progress along the line of a medial centile, in the odd hours of the morning – one o'clock, three, five – when Grace hauled her out of bed for a feed, Theresa thought about the ivy's growth. She had seen the tub at the front of the Master Builder's house. It was hard to believe that such a small beginning should end up so monstrously. Just three stems came out of the pot, hardly sufficient to feed the ivy on all the houses. Bit by bit she gathered in information about the ivy, that the leaves took in the sun's energy and fed the plant, that in times of drought the ivy sucked the moisture out of the walls. One person who shared her hatred of the ivy (not from the street) told her not to look on the internet for information. Everybody there said you couldn't kill ivy, you just had to live with it. Other neighbours, proud of the ivy, talked of how it brought the houses and people together, it was eco, their lives organic. One joked that there was more plant than brick, and that if you removed the ivy the houses would crumble. Another agreed that the ratio of plant to brick was in the former's favour, but believed the brick could be removed to leave houses made of ivy. Another said that their type of ivy was rare, native to South Yorkshire and North Derbyshire, taking refuge, and that the amount of ivy had passed a necessary tipping point some time around the Suez Crisis, and so each house had its own self-sustaining microclimate which meant that none of the ivy needed the tub to survive. At these times of night as the baby suckled and drank her dry, Theresa would fall into a half sleep and confuse Grace with the ivy, insatiable in their need for nutrients. And here she saw how the ivy was forcing its way through the small window frame. It must also be forcing its way through the walls, and she started to fear for Grace. Like the ivy, she had an inkling that Grace was forcing her way in to Theresa's life, growing, growing, growing, and in the night this was at Theresa's expense. Each morning though, in the newly bright April light as it were, things returned to normal, except for her terror of the night, and looking up at the house from the outside, with her back set against the univied houses across the road, it was too much, too much. There came a point when daytime had little reality and it was the nights which had her full attention.

Dinky noticed little in the year. Having saved Theresa, having helped to produce Grace, still with the cushion of money from Theresa's paediatrician sister in London which had helped them buy the house with some to spare to live on until they got themselves established, Dinky was sure he had done enough for now and that all was well in the world of casual labour. He was conscientious when he got the work, but he never sought it. Theresa alternated between irritable and quiet, and in his sensitive way Dinky made allowances for the new mother. He was often out now with his new friend Pete, and the more Theresa told Dinky the ivy had to come down the more he was out drinking. The money wasn't an issue as yet. Knowing it would catch them out, Theresa urged him to get steadier work, or to work more steadily. In his own quiet way he resisted, saying there wasn't much work about, or it didn't pay well, or the weather was against them. Theresa began to spend the days as well as the nights in the attic, obsessing over the ivy. And now there was no difference between the days and the nights. With Dinky seeing Pete, Theresa left to her own devices brooded on the ivy inside the house as it began to replace the wallpaper. She kept the door to the room shut so that Dinky wouldn't see the ivy inside, or rather, kept it shut in case he claimed he couldn't see any ivy and so wouldn't have to do anything about it. The ivy on the outside should be enough to convince him things had to change, she didn't have to convince him it had invaded the interior. She wanted the ivy dead, certainly, and yet, beyond this, she feared it had become a part of her, and the room, and the baby. If she killed the ivy perhaps all of these things would die. But above all, she wanted to kill the ivy.

One day Dinky came back mid-afternoon with Pete after their lunchtime drinking session. Pete liked road movies. He said they were pure nostalgia because the world was killing the car, and there would be a time when there were no cars, then where will we be?, we'll be sorry. He'd got hold of 'Vanishing Point' and waved the dvd case at this inhospitable world as he climbed the hill and was struck and amazed when he realised the whole half-street was ivied. He'd heard tell but this beat all and then Dinky couldn't stand it any longer and let it all out, bewailing Theresa's withdrawal to 'The Room', her banging on about the ivy, wanting him to get shot of it.

The whole thing amused Pete. He worked nights stacking shelves and guessed why Theresa shut herself away when the dark was outside, the sense of your own active world enclosed womb-like against the becalmed world outside. He'd get back, sleep for a few hours, drink, sleep it off, go to work stacking shelves in the middle of the night and then come back again to sleep, to drink, to sleep, to work, what he thought of as an agricultural rhythm for no good reason. This, he intimated to himself, must be Theresa's parallel routine. His friend looked distraught. Pete asked why he didn't take the ivy down. Dinky, after the two of them staring like tipsy love-fools at the ivy for half-an-hour, confessed he had a fear of ladders. Nearly all the work he could do involved ladders, which was why he didn't really get much work. There was always some time when they expected him to go up a ladder, and he wouldn't, he couldn't. Theresa had started to tell him to 'man up' whenever he shirked a job, a phrase she'd picked up from near Barnsley, and this should be her red rag to his bull. He told Pete he thought the ivy had got into her brain, on it, in it, instead of dendrites there were tendrils, Dinky'd looked it up on the net to see if ivy could grow in your head and the ivyhead site made it clear that the connections in the brain were to all intents and purposes ivy, or at least ivy-like. Pete died laughing.

Now that Pete wouldn't take Dinky seriously as a man, Dinky had a waking dream in which he conquered his fear. So he got hold of ladders from someone down the road, and refusing all help, decided to work from the top down, from the guttering where it was pushing out the tiles on the roof. As he was establishing the feet of the ladder on the ground his immediate neighbour came out. Known to Theresa and Dinky as 'Miserable Man', he had never exchanged a single greeting. He asked Dinky what he was doing. Dinky was proud of himself for doing what he was doing, even if he hadn't done anything yet other than get a set of ladders, and confidently told Miserable Man that he was removing the ivy. Miserable Man said he couldn't because it was in the deeds of all their houses, handed down for a century as the Master Builder's bequest. Dinky didn't care, it was ruining his life and making his partner and child ill. It was his house and the ivy had to come down. It had got inside the house Theresa said and it was eating away at her. Theresa came out and gave Miserable Man what for, something she'd been desperate to do since day one when he didn't return her new-to-the-area smile. Pete (another Pete) from the opposite house came over and put in his two-pennyworth.

To escape the brouhaha Dinky Taylor climbed to the top of the ladder. He could see right across the town, picking out mosques and churches, high-rise apartments and the hospital. The whole wide world was before him. Looking down he could see Theresa holding Grace and a small crowd of neighbours. On the wall was the lushness of ivy, varnished mottled green leaves stuck to woody dendrites. He tugged at the nearest branch and was astonished at how tightly it was fixed to the wall. It would take a relatively long time to finish the job. He knew he could do it. Down below they watched, Theresa proud of how he'd manned up and the baby.

Theresa phoned her sister the paediatrician in London as twilight drifted in. She told her that she wouldn't believe the fantastic story she was about to tell her, about Dinky up the ladder, clinging to the ivy as if the ladder wasn't there, as if he had become part of the ivy, his hands and feet clamped on fast, like Grace's gums at the end of her breasts. She told her she had to come to see them, to see Dinky, King of the Ivy, and to see the baby who she hadn't seen to this day. Dinky stared out across the town, astonished to be watching at just the moment somebody switched on all the street lights to replace the light of the sun. Theresa insisted her sister come up to see the baby, it wasn't right that a paediatrician refused to see her own niece, as if she weren't interested in kin, and Theresa proudly told her sister again and again of how Dinky was still working on the wall outside, this time of night.

JB in 1968

JB is having his own crisis – he has been contacted by a former love interest in England. He remembers her as his English Rose, from a time when he was trying so very hard to understand the English. 'You are from the upper middle class – is this accurate?'

Mary Anne is having some kind of crisis of her own, this being the last Wednesday of May 1968, and has got the message to Johannes early that morning to come to the Potteries. He is caught between staying in Paris to be part of unfolding events and being overwhelmed by the immediate and graphic remembrance of seeing Mary Anne for the first time in her underwear in 1953, sporting flimsy white cotton bra and panties with pink and red roses floating delicately, decorously, deliciously, over her breasts and pubis. Who could forget? (he asks me, who never knew). We head to Stoke-upon-Trent to relive that moment and so abandon Paris to her mostly symbolic fate. JB tells me that the world's implosion is the consequence of 'structural violence'. Does he really tell me that? It's not in my copious notes from that very year: 'Americans still reeling from Tet – will they ever recover'; 'Joho – overtaken by . . . himself?'; 'the Czechs have shown the way – Adios Stalin!'. And of course, as if History were writing me!, I have my own crisis. Is this really a job, following Johannes Boanerges for his sole behoof, there to record his every thought? What am I getting out of it? The wages of a Secretary are? Secretary to . . .? One of the greatest of all men – that's all! Yet, and yet, am I nothing other than a gentleman's companion of old while the world moves on and away from me? The philosopher's side-kick, stuck in the cave, in the shadows?

I still carry to this day my Letter of Introduction — just in case things fall through.

I raise the issue with him on the train out of London. He is in gnomic mood, no doubt conjuring up Mary Anne and her skimpy underwear in his mind's eye. 'Seek the wasp and you shall find the wasp' is all he will say, flicking at me that damned Johnsonian orange peel he digs out of his jacket pocket and which I am to dispose of. I am his housekeeper Victor(ia) before Victor(ia) appears. Does he want me to ask about Mary Anne, or to leave him alone? I have no idea who Mary Anne is, not really, other than through one of the phrases he tries out on me: 'she was a young sculptress who fell under my spell'; at other times 'she is an English Rose (pause) who fell under my spell'. Is? Was? Will be? Did *she* fall, or did *he*? Where are we? No doubt in 1968, the twenty-ninth day in May, the beginning of my troubles with JB — a man who insists on moral rectitude, a man who insists on humanity and being humane . . . a man turning his back on the turning tide of history for the memory of a woman . . . a man, just like any other man . . . so what am I doing following him, unable to motivate my own life? I need to break free from JB's tyranny, I need to transform *myself*, not watch an idol show himself to be a damned fool. But, as I've said time and again, this isn't about me. I'm trying to give you the 'full package', JB 'in-the-round'.

So I ask him what is going on. 'Seek the wasp and you will find the wasp' he says, chucking orange peel at my face. We have been too long together it occurs to me. If I had been absent from his mind all this time like she had, would he think of me as fondly? But I do not have flimsy underwear, my underwear is sturdy, one man's string vest is never appealing to another man, I am no English rose. We have been too long together, Johannes and I, and I am losing my life to him, sacrificing my life to him. This cannot, should not be. Mary Anne is the same age as I am, so, some twenty years younger than the esteemed man of . . . We are in the same position perhaps, she and I, caught up in the lure of genius. Is Johannes the wasp? Is that what he means? In his hieratic manner has he gone to the heart of the matter and told me more about myself than I could have discovered *by* myself? 'Seek the wasp . . . and be stung by the wasp'? And now perhaps he seeks his own wasp? I want to chuck the orange peel back in his face, and in fact do so. He looks up at me, puzzled, upset, uninterested in me, I can see that. 'You are jealous of Mary Anne!', he laughs, looks out the window at the flat English country-side. Sometimes I think he has a middle-European laugh and he is not Livonian or Smyrnan (if that's what they are called), and so sometimes I think he sees the lives of others as caught up in a cruel folk tale, with stones in our bellies and crows to peck out our eyes. I want to ask him what he is thinking. He does not like English trains he says, and he has given up trying to understand the English for he declares: 'there is nothing to understand, they have morals but are not moral, they have shaped the world without understanding the world. That is why they will now lose the world, have already lost it. Pah! Nations states!'

For the umpteenth time he gets out his comb and rakes his hair in the window's reflection. What will it behove him to have a tidy crop? He can't really think that this adventure will be the rekindling with a woman twenty years his junior. It is true that he knows many women in many cities, and he has his amorous ways, he has his charisma, he has that. It is true. Perhaps I am wrong about everything.

'You are turning your back on Europe just at the time of *the revolution*', I mock.

'Yes, I am a man'.

'And . . .? Let's go back to Paris, Joho. What will your students think? They will be preparing for your class, sorry, teach-in. They will be expecting you, the great man, to inspire them, to provoke them in thought and deed. Some Union men are coming as well – there has never been a time when intellectuals and the working class have joined hands like this. If you do not go back there will be nothing, no guidance from you and the revolution will fail. And for what? Some *femme fatale*!'

'You talk nonsense. A friend says she is having a crisis, I cannot abandon her, I have to rush to her with all speed. There is nothing else to be done. It is "the realm of chance in the realm of necessity", as your man says'.

'You mean you cannot abandon a vision of her bra and panties!' The others in the carriage, making their way out of the capital like us, give old-fashioned looks but say nothing. Hushed, 'you have abandoned the world for your . . . for your . . .', and I nod towards his groin. I have gone too far. Or not far enough.

We get off the train, JB tremendously anxious. And for me it's awful to have 'what am I doing here?' going through my head every single minute, but I can't help it. Stoke! How have I ended up in Stoke? Ceramics – Lordy, whatever next? If there's one branch of art that has no place in my heart, it's pottery. A plate is a plate is a plate.

'Do you see her, Joho? If not, shall we take the return to London?' Somebody stops near us and starts staring. 'Is this her, I ask you?'

JB isn't looking in her direction, so I grab hold of his face asking myself 'what am I doing here in Stoke guessing if this is the woman JB remembers?' and forcibly get him to stare back at the woman. 'No', the great man says and turns away. The woman continues to stare and JB isn't as unaware as you might think and feels the force of the woman's gaze boring into him, objectifying him, making him stiffen up. As he turns to face the gaze of the starey woman a man a good couple of feet away from her starts to stare at Joho as well. Something is amiss, clearly, some kind of platform incident in the making. 'This is the hub of North Staffordshire', I tell him, hoping to ease the situation, when a couple join the woman and the man and stand and stare at my man. 'Let's make for the Exit, she must be meeting us there. I have the tickets'.

'Qu'est-ce qu'elles foutent?' JB has reverted to swearing in French, as he often does when he wants to have a go at the English. This creates a minor ripple amid what can only now be described as a small crowd of people surrounding us in a curious fashion. 'C'est quoi ce bordel sont-ils regardaient?' That gets them going again, and there is now a mass with people actively standing on tip-toe at the back.

'I really cannot say JB what the fuck they are staring at' (whispered, in English), 'but we are a little too near the edge of the platform and they are losing inhibitions, and if they press any closer we will have a right old putain de crise, if you will pardon my French'.

The Stoke crowd is a motley crew, and all we can hear is 'duck', and an undertow of 'conk' and 'French' and 'him' and 'missing' and 'cowardy cowardy custard' and of course!:

'Joho – they think you're the great asparagus', and I can't stop laughing.

'de Gaulle. They think I am de Gaulle? Quelle baise joue! Does this look like de Gaulle?', he shouts at them, turning sideways, pointing to his nose, 'is this the nose of a de Gaulle?' The Stokeites are not convinced, because JB's nose – though nobody would say this to his nose – is rather noteworthy. 'I am *not Charles de Gaulle*! Look – *his* nose' (holds his hands wide apart) '*my* nose' (closes his hands up to a width some way short of the true measure).

I shout for the Guard, who pushes his way through to us. 'We've been looking for you!' There is a chorus of 'told you so' and the odd 'get back to France' and a lone 'we're going to miss the match'.

'I am not Charles de Gaulle!'

'He would say that, wouldn't he?', says the first woman who appeared, a look of smug disdain, 'he *would* say *that*!'

'Are you John Boggans? John Gobbaknees?'

'Johannes Boanerges. Yes'.

'Come with me Sir', and the full authority of a British uniform takes Johannes by the arm and leads him and me through a crowd which believes Charles de Gaulle has debunked from governing France to seek anonymous succour in his beloved Stoke-upon-Trent, only to find himself recognised because the nose is the one body part that cannot be disguised, and to find himself arrested by the Transport Police. With every step and retelling the crowd increases the size of his proboscis so by the time we get to the station foyer his conk is the size of Staffordshire and we are its inhabitants, grubbing around for ingress and egress, along with all the other pottery ducks.

And there she is, a vision of . . . somebody who smokes and drinks heavily and discovers themselves to be fifty. *That's* a *crisis*, deary. Whatever image of loveliness he had in his head, it certainly wasn't this jowelly, tired-looking hag, ordering him to come closer so she can get a good look at what once was. *He* certainly won't be wanting a closer look at *her*. Oh, for Pity's Sake, *will he*? There's no European kiss, but instead she grips a head that has been on this planet for nigh on seventy years stock still in her hands, nicotine-yellow fingers over his crinkled, hairy ears, and plants her oversized lips full on his over-ripe lips with as much passion as a teenage girl (his lips don't appear to have been dried out by the twentieth century, nor her ardour). Not to be outdone, once she's let him come up for air, he grabs her head back, and ups the ante, forcing in a tongue that has helped him eat more hot dinners than . . . I give up. A new crowd begins to stand and stare, male gaze, female gaze, stock gaze, Stoke

142

gaze. Is it the age gap (a disgusting twenty years) is it the passion (?) is it the sixties? Is this the outward sign of crisis, because tomorrow they (we) die? Or is it the life force shining through, breaking beyond the hidden codes of authority and tradition? Are they showing Stoke another way? Some of the new crowd who were part of the old crowd haven't forgiven him for either (a) being de Gaulle or (b) pretending to be de Gaulle. There is genuine revulsion at his French male behaviour (he's French either way), coming over the Channel to steal English roses, and there are muttered moans about idle students, and some in the crowd who know Mary Anne who are puzzled or impressed, depending on who they think Johannes is (she's snogging the French President!). It's five o'clock.

Six o'clock

Tea chez Mary Anne. This consists mainly of cigarettes and vodka in her studio. We sit on benches. JB drools. A large part of the studio – a converted attic in a large crumbly Victorian house – is covered by acres of dirty sheets with 'Tet', 'Offensive', 'Socialism', 'Crisis', 'One dimensional', 'Human Face' scrawled on in large block capitals. She explains that these mean nothing, they were given to her when she needed large sheets to cover . . . 'That's why I wanted you here, Joey. My masterpiece lies under those sheets. Ignore the writing, that means nothing. But I'm too close to it, and an artist needs distance, Joey, distance!, distance!, and who has been more distant than you? It's why I need you – I need your distant eye, your distant mind, the fact you are far away in time and space'.

What world was she looking out onto? She looked like she needed something quite desperately, while her Joey was about to hit seventy. The younger woman would kill the poor man. I really had to protect him from her, didn't I? Or perhaps I could finally break free, and leave him to gallivant – if that's what it was – in Stoke. The great man, the great thinker, the great optimistic sceptic. And our tea (hardly dinner?) A baked potato and a bit of cheese and a brick of butter. Either Mary Anne couldn't cook, or she was struggling financially, or she was both, which was the most likely. Behind JB was 'Offensive' and behind Mary Anne was 'Crisis'. With plates on the floor they started cooing again, sharing smoke rings, sucking fingers. I cleared my throat and was told where the bathroom was, not that I'd asked. I stayed. She couldn't be allowed to besmirch JB. I repeat: she would have killed him.

Seven o'clock

We make our way to a collection of rectangular buildings on foot from the attic, to the specific rectangular building where Mary Anne teaches. JB doesn't look great – I believe he's been sick – it's been a few years since he's inhaled so much smoke. The room echoes with the clatter of chair legs when we re-arrange the seating. It's the studio where Mary Anne teaches and the students start to drift in, seven for seven thirty, all female apart from a couple of young lads. She chats with them about their latest adventures in sexland and the fine arts and now JB is out of her compass he looks on despondently and is forced to speak to me as if he knows me, in a low voice at the front of the class.

'I'm in love, all over again. Isn't it marvellous? She hasn't changed one bit?'

'You mean she's always looked like a hag?'

'Now now, my jealous male secretary, not nice. I want you to record this teach-in and then to make notes of the sculpture Mary Anne will let us see later on. She's been working on it for three years, maybe longer. Cigarette? Light? She won't say too much about it, she doesn't want to colour my judgment. I need to sit down. Get me a chair – where am I sitting? – Mary Anne, where am I sitting? – she can't hear me – the students adore her, you can tell – not a bad turn out – about forty – it's short notice of course – there's another meeting on for Biafra – do you think I should mention that? – what's the matter?, you're sulking – look, Paris is Paris and here is here, you seek the wasp . . . she is my English Rose, my beautiful English Rose, she is in my heart, do you see? – you must understand, and not think of us as foolish old people – in our hearts, *our hearts* . . . get me a chair, quick, and some water'. He hasn't groomed in a while and so the bad part of me focuses on his unsavoury ears and nostrils.

The room is large enough for about forty people amid the paraphernalia of art, pictures for inspiration, tubes of paint, a kiln, modelling clay and clay clay, easels, books of the artists, a blackboard divided down the middle into 'Form' and 'Content' with arrows urgently communicating between the two.

'Is it all girls, Mary Anne?'

'They are women, you sexist pig. There is a football match on, I have no

144

idea what, quite important I'm told. "Best Nobby"? Is that male slang? Now, let's wind up our – my – genius and set him running. Doesn't he look distinguished? A bit like de Gaulle? Fancy running off and not telling a body! And you're the one in charge of the country?! That's class, Joey, that's class!'

Seven thirty

Johannes is not inspired, and in fact looks decidedly ill and ill-at-ease. His opening sally, subscribing to the theory that you open with a joke and keep it local or topical, is 'hello, my lovely ducks', which is met with embarrassment. To win them round he praises Mary Anne, and this does the trick, for thirty seconds. He mentions 'structural violence' and the need for revolt. They nod with puzzled faces. He mentions the tragedy unfolding in Biafra. They nod with puzzled faces. Why have they come? He says the problem with the West, with all of us, is that we are too comfortable. The audience shifts in its plastic seats. I note this down, look over to Mary Anne who is oblivious to how badly this is going because she is in awe of her Joey (on this performance?) and I note this down in exactly the same words – 'Mary Anne is oblivious . . .'. She has told them to expect the second coming and instead they get a ponderous dry-as-dust who has misjudged his audience, their values, and himself.

'The centre cannot hold', he says, plucked from his canon of prophecies, and he leaves it to echo round the room. For extra significance he repeats it. And all it does is echo. He has to repeat it a third time, to make sure the centre does not hold. Their centre of indifference holds, so he starts on one of his other riffs. 'A strong man will emerge. Democracy has failed. This time the strong man will be benignly ruthless – yes, this is the truth. "Seek the wasp and you shall find the wasp". What people do not understand is that democracy and capitalism are *necessary* to each other. We are comfortable, I am comfortable, you here are comfortable [there is hostile bum-movement] and democracy means the ruling bourgeois thirty-per-cent legitimate their power over us. This is not democracy, it is *the failure of democracy*, democracy in any true sense [contradicting, it has to be said, although nobody really notices, his published work castigating the very idea that democracy is ever viable or truly desirable, and his unambiguous, unproduced play from the end of the 50s, *The Last Timid Conviction*]. I agree with my good friend Herbert [JB continues] – Herbert Marcuse – Herbert Marcuse? [in despair at the

145

crowd's ignorance] Herbert Marcuse, *One Dimensional Man*?, come on, you must have read *One Dimensional Man*? You've *truly* not *read* it? [he continues regardless, in for a penny, in for . . .] I agree with him that the old class antagonisms have been reconciled, and so we are *comfortable* – can you stop fidging, fudging, what's that idiom?, ah, can you stop *fidgeting* every time I say *comfortable*? – and that *we* are one-dimensional. But believe me, forget all about this Cold War conspiracy, forgot about dreams of atomic bombs and apocalypse and zero sums and nuclear winters, forgot about these foolish things and focus on real change, not the change of your sexy zeitgeist, your sexy time-ghost is nothing more than superficial youthful posturing, nothing more, it does not represent the underlying historical trend of our overheated century, which is the failure of democracy and the need to present, by force if necessary, a new texture to being, to social relations, to consciousness, to our human health, the deep well of humanity'.

And with that and many other flights of language which I won't recount here [more of the same] JB has at last succeeded in hypnotising the group. It was not necessary to follow the logic of any argument – you felt you had it, then it disappeared as soon as you stared it in the eye, but didn't care because the music carried on sounding in your very soul – it was only necessary to let the beauty of his voice and his lyric of the human – which was his alone – enter the better part of yourself and JB held their hands metaphorically as he now held Mary Anne's literally and ushered us towards greener grass. Even the two lads listening to the match – now forty minutes in, 8.25 p.m., without incident, were Best and Charlton failing?, was Eusabio too good? – were smitten. *Now, now* they could see what the fuss was about – the man embodied the whole of history, literature, philosophy and politics – you looked at him and felt how profoundly you understood the hidden powers that controlled your life, the lives of your parents, friends, enemies, the downtrodden of nation states, and how you might defeat these omnipotencies. There was nothing he didn't know, there was nothing of the twentieth century that he hadn't seen, and there was nothing you wouldn't do for him. I, too, felt what they felt and I saw what they saw. He had experienced history, been present at its key moments, known the horrors, and had the strength to hold himself together, expand, explain, interpret, foretell, the master of global exegesis. Mary Anne beamed and kissed.

How could either of us refuse him?

146

The drunker we became in the pub, the more visible were the hidden powers of the universe. Upstairs at Mary Anne's, accompanied by a smattering of student acolytes and a never-ending supply of vodka and cigarettes, we sat where we could. Mary Anne said she would reveal everything, and I think Joho expected a private showing, but the struggle, so she told us, ready to lift the veil, was with form and function, form and content, to make art political and still be art, to make history the present and still be history, to represent . . . and so on (noted down as such under my heading 'The Ideal City').

May 29, 1968, midnight, Stoke, *The Ideal City*

That oversexed minor British sculptress and well-known lush Ms Heply shows us her juvenile creation which she calls 'The Ideal City'. It is all white, buildings made out of words and phrases (I write as I observe; it's made out of lego and cardboard). She is as drunk as a skunk, getting drunker, getting smellier skunkier to do it and she has to get us just as drunk and skunk-like to 'appreciate' her nonsense. The phrases are revolutionary. Does Ms Heply hope to cause a revolution? An arch in front of a round building says 'desormais'. Arch indeed. All I can say is '*henceforth*, no more, thank you'. If ever a revolutionary work of art did no justice to art or revolution, I am looking at it. More vodka will help me see more clearly. 'Mary Anne, more vodka please!'

***

Boanerges, Johannes, 'The Ideal City: Heply's Revolution', *Architecture* 10.2 (July) 1968.

SPACE

THE BOURGEOISIE OWN SPACE

We know they have commandeered time: clock discipline. Clock in, clock out. You have one day out of seven for you (*to prepare for the next six – leisure* on the Saturday? – *you PAY for your leisure – it belongs to the cash nexus – it supports the economy that doesn't support you*). You have ten days each year – we count, we give, you thank us – for holiday (*to ease the pain for the next year*). Round and round you go on the carousel, work-to-live, live-to-work, work-to-live, live-to-work, work-to . . .

WE DID NOT KNOW THEY OWN SPACE

Space. It is a sign of the overwhelming nature of industrial capitalism that it owns all space on the planet. Not land, this is much more than mere 'land', so much more, this is fundamental, as fundamental as time.

The bourgeoisie own space. They own many things. The source of their power is not the ownership of the means of production, though this is important.

In the Eighteenth Century the bourgeois class incloses space. Now it is enshrined. Now it is the foundations of their very existence.

TAKE TO THE STREETS

Revolution takes to the streets: reclaims space. People, the masses, the twentieth century, 1968, must take to the streets to reclaim space. Paris: alignment of buildings. Boulevards – the space between buildings where we are free to roam when they let us, when they don't put their tanks there. The buildings *cost*. Paris aligns its buildings, restricts their height, controls and limits space *above the ground*. It disciplines space as the masters discipline time. Who would think you could enclose *air* as well as *land*? It has been thought. They have thought it. It is handed down. *Property* – what is a *proper tie* for them: the enclosure of space with property. Haussman and Wren – architect collaborators (no doubt) – a house man and a bird.

The streets are a clarion call – in the middle of a street we see the space corralled by bricks and mortar, space that cannot be ours, space that once belonged to no-one, space that climbs fifty metres, one hundred metres, above the ground – how is it somebody puts a stone fence around airy emptiness and calls it theirs and sells it. Empty space. For sale. ***THE STREETS MUST BE OURS***

THE IDEAL CITY

Mary Anne Heply's 'Ideal City' is constructed from the slogans and graffiti that define our now, the historical now, not the fashionable now, but the political now crafted by the industrial-military complex, by the comfortable phase of capitalism, by the Cold War that keeps us warm, because *we know* (don't we?) that no leader would be MAD enough?

Everyone talks of crisis. Heply does more, as every great artist should: Heply fuses past, present, future. The future is part of now, but it takes Heply's imagination to show us. Heply *re-fuses* past, present, future. She refuses. This is the nature of crisis.

It is not a crisis, she has decided – she has moved beyond that – it is an epiphany, for her, for us, *for me*. She calls this work 'View of the Ideal City', reference to the fifteenth-century 'The City of God'. Need I say more?

Each building crafted in the raw from the slogans and graffiti that define our now. Each word, each utterance, lays bare the ugly accretion of our domination, how we have allowed ourselves to be dominated through our ceding of space. You own space – by force, by religion (*the city of GOD*), by military might – and then you can exclude, then you can pen in those who belong not.

They are ***white***. Need I say more? Empire collapses.

White is not an ideal colour. Heply knows this. Race and architecture.

Sculpture is white. Sculpture and race.

In the centre a circular shrine, two stories. Around the top 'DESORMAIS'

Meaning: Henceforth, this city which is not ours will be differently known. It is not natural. We cognise. Do you cognise?

The pillars in the shrine, at random: 'I AM YEAST NOT BREAD' 'CONCRETE BREEDS APATHY' 'QUICK! THERE'S JUST TIME' 'UNDER THE PAVING STONES THERE IS THE BEACH' 'TOTAL ORGASM MAN' 'NO LETS! OCCUPY POLITICS'

I here add my own columns: 'THE COURAGE NOT TO BUILD' 'REFUSE SPACE'

Imagine the city springs forth from the streets, from the slogans of our mind.

Mary Anne Heply is that conduit, the channel for history, for politics, for spirit, feels the interplay of body, space, fusion of sculpture-architecture. The city is the visible sign of crisis.

There are no humans in 'The City of God'; there are no humans in Heply's slogan city. The unwritten, the unsaid is megaphoned – there can be no human face until the revolution has succeeded. There can be no humane space until capitalism and imperialism and colonialism are ruined absolutely'.

The piece continues, lists more slogans, goes nowhere. You should look up his piece for *Time* of the same year: that's more in keeping with Johannes Boanerges, makes more sense, less caught up in all that nonsense about 'space'; 'space' – just because he had nothing of substance to say about the Hag's Bag o' Bricks.

The whole Friday morning (Thursday was a hangover washout: de Gaulle had returned for a start, and some of the acolytes just wouldn't leave) I could see that JB was sexually frustrated – his mouth purses and his lips flare and he's quick to anger and he talks of bees not wasps. When we left Mary Anne at Stoke station, I managed to linger in earshot and heard something from her throaty voice about his lack of movement on women, 'like the rest of the fucking socialists'. The leaving kisses were on cheeks only and she gave him a gift package. My sense of satisfaction was complete when I found she had plied him with a copy of 'Women: The Longest Revolution', 'The Radical Women Manifesto' and *The Golden Notebook*. His instructions were to read and understand. If he could reform (Mary Anne said, as he related to me a few years later) she would give up misandry and see him again on equal terms. He thought she was joking. Maybe she was, but it was not that kind of joke, it was a new kind of joke he couldn't understand. What really cut him though was being given *The Human Situation: A Feminine View*, for *he*, Johannes Boanerges, was master of 'the human', defining 'the human' was *his* domain. How could there be another view that wasn't defined by him, that didn't defer to his ideas? None of it made sense.

And that probably accounts for his piece in *Time* in August which selects those parts of 1968 he approves of and those he castigates. Revolution, yes; hedonism, no (I sensed once more a seriousness that was born of Europe, not America). Decolonisation, yes; democracy, no no no. The article, and JB, were universally reviled. He had missed Paris at a crucial time, and his groin had missed out on a set of white cotton bra and panties from 1953 sporting pink and red floral motifs. JB, as he realised to his own chagrin, was out of step and out of luck.

May 38th

Back in Paris I start my own magazine. JB will fund *May 38TH*, bless him, the title marking the very day that I have that very brilliant idea of starting my own magazine, just before my 50th birthday. The start-up money is his way of saying 'sorry' to me, his loyal Boswell, 'sorry' to the Paris he abandoned, 'sorry' to those on the barricades (who were bankers the next year). I ask JB to write the *Foreword* to *May 38TH's* first issue. It begins: 'Every man wants to watch another man die. This is how history begins. This is how history ends. Hegel states . . .'

The Champagne Bar

A penchant for upmarket hotel drinking has always been with us. Temporary settlements for voyagers, furniture, lobby, theme, staff with masks, the wide open spaces expense pays for, location in the city's best sector, deep rich seats and secreted booths, large decorative features from hip young designers constructed innovative materials, old-school illuminated perspex changes colour, shape, significance. We would never buy champagne, we only end up here after visiting theatres or cinemas or restaurants.

My wife goes to the toilet hoping to meet a famous woman rearranging her face in the wide mirror, or found distraught on speaker phone, just in time to comfort her. We are recently married. We leave our coats to mark territory, me walking up to the bar, I've done all that before, it feels similar. About twice I have chatted with Andrea – he is here from Rumania for many years. Single, not like us. This could be the first time now, another time. They are all similar. If I had paid more attention to the changing sofas . . . the bar itself hasn't changed, the lighting has changed through the seasons. 'Did you always serve champagne?' He is a trained mixologist, trained in Holland, tells the two smart-dressed men who haven't asked the history of cocktails. The word 'vermouth' is exciting; he uses a small spiral stick that's not been seen before we all watch him build the drink. The trade secret for this drink is the difference in viscosity for three liquids. Vermouth. Towards the mouth he says from on high. The men are not cocktailers, these are the cocktails we give to others, and they order American craft beers, move away, sit down with elegant hearts, similar.

Andrea completes the order, puts the drinks on a tray with unusual nuts, comes from behind the bar, goes over to the men and their other halves. How long before I get to order is unknown, similar. I am not a good waiter, look over to our coats in the booth still there, the card-trick man hovers. Will we let him come to us? He starts out smoothly, always, and after three tricks folds into the patter his dead friend. Does the hotel employ him to do this? Does the hotel know how poorly it can sit with the clientele?

Is it possible to get cake this time of night? Terri, my wife, wants cake at this time of night, has a craving. I try not to judge her against the other times and the other people, watching Andrea collect glasses. There are two members of staff visible through the door ajar abutting the shifting perspex prosing in the manner appropriate to a late night hotel bar. I really would like to shout to them that I'm not being served, or to give Andrea another couple of minutes. The woman I've seen before and has a name beginning with L. She emerges for something else, her name begins with Ks, Ksenia the badge says, and I ask if I can order some drinks. 'What are you talking about with the staff?' Her look is extremely not committed so I ask about the cake, if it is possible to have cake, you serve it in the afternoon as afternoon tea on pretty blue-striped tiered cake-stands, perhaps there are evening fancies and alcohol you could purvey. She will go off to ask the man standing through the door ajar and disappears into the back. As far as I am concerned I have put in the order and walk back to our booth, similar like before, with the restaurant in the background and the verbiage in the abutting Winter Garden majestic, delightful, green.

Before Terri went to the Ladies Room to look at the skin on her face and we were together in the champagne bar I had never been more knowingly at peace. Now Terri is off somewhere there is a grim ambience and my gulping starts, for air, for drink, for reward. The magician, thin, haunted, full head of hair, plausible enough, won't approach me if I'm alone. In the restaurant the noise from the wedding party rises – it is a strange, public place to enjoy the closing chapter of your celebrations – the noise is indistinct and they lack most communication, bodies with heads seen from this vantage point, repeated.

Andrea is returned behind the bar taking another order while making up another order. He is always doing this. Ksenia and the other man join him and infrequently they speak, Ksenia indicating with that lift of her head my direction and that something needs to be done I hope. The unknown third man comes out from behind the bar and moves in my direction to get more

153

cake details misses me altogether heads in the direction of reception round the corner where I can't see him. He is needed there. The other times have been very similar to this, very similar, when a person approaches me, a waiter or Terri, and the world is regrooved, back to its origin. The magician has disappeared, and Andrea and Andrea and Andrea.

It is easy to think of all the reasons my wife isn't there here back from the famous toilet, for Andrea and Ksenia will understand as I work my way through them, and the third man even if he joins us. What is harder to fathom is the lack of a fulfilled order. 'Andrea!' My voice won't carry beyond the first table, a mother and daughter combination, wedded to each other, to each other's life, startled by my anguish. This, this has been seen many times. There are some occasions in the younger woman's past when things haven't worked out and she has ended back at the house of her mother. The father is out with his golfing cronies, or has left, or is dead. Mother and daughter, in the champagne bar shackles very much so.

If only Terri would come back from the toilet.

She returns as the cake and the drinks arrive. 'Hello wife!'

'I love this place', she says, 'love it!'

The magician appears, smiling, 'do you mind if I show you a card trick?', we know what's coming, and happily let him begin his patter. He hails from Mexborough, and after the third card trick his dead friend appears and there is a homily on friendship which we agree with, signalling to him that it is time for him to leave us be two once more. 'Like all the other times'. The mechanical grand piano starts up.

II

The colours scroll through pastel rainbow changing time and symbol behind the new waiter. At the place where you wait to be seated for the restaurant is another vertical slab of light, shifting under water. The toilets sit to the side of the light, huge on the inside, memorable. We came straight past reception, through the emptying lobby, into the champagne bar. This is another 'for once', order a bottle to sit in an ice bucket. The restaurant over the way is where we have just emerged from, their toilets not bad not the best. 'I love the toilets here', says Terri, 'best pop to the loo'. 'I'll see if they have cake'.

We know that we shouldn't be hungry, we know that we aren't hungry. It's our treat here, now that we are recently married. There have been other excuses, very similar excuses, in similar times for eating cake. It's not a good idea, ruins the taste of the wine, though we are not connoisseurs, and never will be. It is part of the charm of being together.

It can be seen. They take orders at the bar, come to your table for orders, the one thing bad form is to insist you take the drinks away from the bar your self – they should be brought to the table, and you should pay by card not cash – don't take the drinks away from the bar is the rule. Nobody says this. You have to come here time and again, notice the pattern of invisible disdain in order to understand. It is not to happen. Terri and I have seen it many times, laughed between ourselves, co-conspirators, secret sharers, soulmates, at the gross iniquities here. Terri reminds me of the time she explained sub rosa to me. Ah, Terri. How I love her! I must stop judging her against the past. Did she appreciate the rose, me holding it above her head, before we came in? Of course, she understood the joke. And inside, before she went to the toilet, I framed the staff and the bar in the distance with some elaborate joshing and then held the rose above the picture. 'Watch!' I said, and we watched the antics of the staff and their masks. The magician, who we often forgot, hove into view, spoilt it, moved on, purveying his lost friend and cards to a very young couple that we did not envy. Then Terri had to pop to the loo, as I remember. We all go to the toilet many times in the course of our lives and when the other is gone and we are alone we can reflect on the city and our happiness. The city allows us to live our life to the full. If only there were more time to be in the city more often late at night. The babysitter waits for us and pressures us by sitting the children when we are out, that's the whole arrangement in a nutshell. Really I would have preferred to go to the cinema to be immersed in sound and light and narrative and people projected in front of us, an escape from food. But no, we went to the restaurant and it will be a while before we can afford again the babysitter remember for next time to insist on the cinema not to compromise to keep your voice don't let it be drowned out by Terri. I love Terri!

Really Terri is the only person I have been to the Champagne Bar with.

One of the other times here I am with people from work after we went to the same restaurant and came here straight after in the same way. These are the kinds of things I think about when on your own because when Terri comes back these memories will fall back into the distant neuronal paths. You move from remembering the similar times to the mechanism for remembering which you don't understand and which you have no control over. That time after explaining sub rosa to me Terri explained neurons and memory to me. I don't like to tell her it makes me sick to the stomach to think my brain is whirring away with neurons chugging out stupid memories and to think that any feelings I have are just neurons not feelings at all. It's really grim. I avoid telling her about things I don't like that she likes.

The bucket has not appeared on the table and the magician approaches the mother and daughter with cards he shifts between hands we thought he wasn't coming back to the hotel because we made a complaint that he depresses us and we love this place, love it to bits. I stare at the rose. It's real, I presume, and check. Terri spends longer and longer in the bathroom and one day – it's funny sad to think it – it will be so long it will be like she hasn't returned and I will be waiting. She will return, of course, but there will be no end to the time she is in the bathroom, going to the toilet, making up, talking to famous people, so that it will seem like she isn't coming back at all. It is just that the time she spends in there will be so long she may as well not be here at all, she may as well not imply that she's coming back, we may as well not be together we are apart for so long we could meet other people to marry. I think I understand now. 'Just wait while I pop to the loo'. 'The bucket isn't here yet' I will say when she returns after a long stint away, and I won't tell her that I had started to worry that something had happened to her because she had been gone so long. 'Where would I go?' she would ask, genuinely puzzled, and then laugh. These are other things that happen time and again, watching Andrea in chopped conversation with the other staff from a good distance in one of the far booths and attempting to work out when it's our turn.

When Terri comes out the toilet door I am chatting to Ksenia only it's not Terri and the woman walks off to the restaurant. There is a new space between the bar and the restaurant where they hold people before seating them and Andrea has to take complimentary unusual nuts or nuts cleverly stuffed with shredded olives. The long thin woman daughter of the long thin mother sympathise with the magician, cards packed away, unsentimental story of dead friend on the table, a distraction from the new holding layout about which we have not been consulted. The player-piano starts up a Chopin nocturne, playing itself with electricity. This too is stored up for when Terri returns. It's never been this long I tell the absent Terri before the order has arrived really never this long before this is really long. Before Terri went to the toilet we were talking about the age we had the children which was late because it was a long time before we realised love had found us out. The magician has disappeared once more leaving the mother and daughter silent. What will they talk about now? The dissipated father? The magician's dead friend? The magician? How their lives always come to this place? Three times we have overheard them talk about their lives, how banal and entangled they are, it is part of what we hope for when we set out for the evening. We made a mistake about the magician and hope he does well since it's certain the hotel does not pay him it suffers him. Without Terri I know I am nothing and have to wait for her to return to be somebody. Before Terri arrived I was waiting for her all my life and then she found me out, made me a target and the irony is waiting for her again each time in the Champagne Bar when before we met I was waiting for her before even knowing she exists. Sometimes, really every time, we come here my desire is to tell Terri how hollowed out I feel and see how she would react to that and see if she would say the same. If she would say the same thing as me we would really be soul-mates living sub-rosa in a world of champagne bar masks! It would be risky. She would worry that I was hollowed out if she didn't feel hollowed out herself and that, I see now, would be a problem, the beginning of many. Will we still come to the champagne bar?

Without tray Ksenia approaches the table and asks me if I would like to order. 'I've already ordered'. 'I will check'. That should do the trick. The advantage of having to wait is that it stretches out the evening, allows us to feel carefree, not worry about hollowing out with repetition, with being this old, with having children late, with having to spend more time in the bathroom, longer visits each time. We're not that old there is a lot of downhill fun to be had.

III

The waitress has her hair pulled back tightly into a bun, because her face is thin and severe it is as if her face is tied back as hair, the flesh gripped backwards from the jaw, back, back, into the bun, so you see the chin bone and all the teeth, and cheeks and vacant eye sockets and nasal cavity. Terri (I imagine) looks in the mirror and sheers the carapace, runs me into one sequence to make me and forgets me when the telestar in full fur falls to pieces, mascara face-trailed, asks for secular forgiveness from our Terri for her betrayal of a friend with another friend that very morning. And she's done it before, she repeats the unforgiveable act, and speaks of addiction to our Terri who could be anybody there, any person who sheers the carapace. The telestar holds friendship in the highest esteem, before trouncing friendship, and Terri tries to comfort the telestar the telestar cannot bear to be touched and Terri it can only be imagined wants to return to me.

The magician hangs around, waiting to make something happen, waiting to talk about his dead friend. I wait for Terri to return from her adventure, stare sub rosa through the skin to the glistening white skull bone. Yes, I think, there is something of his dead friend lurking or lingering on. He hangs back from a young family, the boy swings the girl's cardigan at her face time and again, makes her laugh. This time most people are dressed in inexpensive t-shirts, talk inexpensively as Terri takes her time in the toilet, as I cup the bone of my chin and stroke to aid thought and to ease the pain of waiting again and again for Terri to show up. The strings of an electrical grand piano are its ribs with shins beneath so I could storm the women's toilets when The Minute Waltz starts up. A minute's humiliation I could bear, just that one minute, to kill waiting. One minute. There is no contract between Terri's skull and mine to prevent me storming the women's toilets, nothing, no implication, no social nuance I have missed, catch Andrea's attention, the gristle of his ears, his aftershave. A woman like a telestar trots intact out of the toilets. 'Andréa, where's my order for Terri?' This is similar, like there never has been a first time, like this is skulls in love once and always, similar. And without Terri here with me now in this booth, with Terri inexplicably delayed in the women's toilets, it gets harder not to think the thoughts she keeps at bay, how anybody could reach me through a facial orifice with her hand's long, strong prehensile fingers which can reach through the slime right to the middle of this middle of this middle of this middle and force it all back out, pulling it there, showing my trick to the magician, a coal for Newcastle.

Button

They didn't wait for a birthday and gave it to her when they thought she was old enough. 'Here it is', Zelie's parents said, 'the button' and solemnly handed over an indescribable push-button affair, 'it can do many things good as well as bad, it's for you darling, just for you' and finishing 'you can only press it once in your life. Make a wish and press. Only once mind'.

Her parents weren't like other people's parents, she knew. Her mother had a face like a witch and her father was never well. Neither of them worked, and it wasn't the first odd object they'd given her or the first odd things they'd said. She had to get to school and her friend Marianna would be waiting, so she tucked away the packed lunch and made sure she'd got the completed homework sheet on approximations. By the time she met up with Marianna Zelie had forgotten all about the button.

A man from Thailand came into the school to talk about solving problems. He told them the story of a peasant family whose daughter brought home her fiancé for the first time. 'Fetch some wine' the father tells the daughter and she goes down into the cellar. On the wall is an axe which might fall at any time and kill her fiancé, and so she starts crying, for in her imagination the axe does fall and kill him. The mother who is left upstairs with the others wonders what has happened to her daughter and goes down to the cellar. When the daughter has finished explaining why she is crying the mother sits down and starts crying too, imagining the horrible death of her future son-in-law. Upstairs the father says he had better see what is holding up the wine and apologises. Once he too has heard the story from the women of the axe hanging dangerously on the wall that could kill the fiancé he joins them in crying. The fiancé makes his way down to the cellar because he can hear sobs.

He notices the axe resting dangerously on a loose hook, lifts it off the hook, and places it on the floor against the wall.

'Every problem can be solved', said the guest speaker. What Zelie remembered most was the long pig-tail the man had. She put her hand up when he said the children could ask questions. He didn't know what the answer to the button was and said she should press it and make a wish for the world to be a peace with itself.

After school Zelie went to Marianna's house and in her bedroom started making up stories about the Thai's long pigtail, gave it magic powers. She had her tea with Marianna and they thought of all the things they could do with the button. Marianna's parents were nice and they suggested she ask for world peace.

'If I ask for world peace, does that mean I will be able to always do my math's homework? When I can't do my homework there's never any peace, I'm not even joking, so if I ask for world peace that must mean I can finish my homework, doesn't it?'

'Yes', said Marianna's mother and Zelie forgot all about the push-button once more and when she got home nobody mentioned it.

***

When Zelie came of age the parents were little changed and Zelie had suppressed as best she could the idea that something special would be given to her. Her father was confined to his bed and her mother spent most of her time tending him, more witch-like than ever so that grown-up Zelie had become afraid of her. There were no presents, and Zelie accepted that although she had come of age her place in the house was little changed. 'Don't forget the button', her mother said, 'it's in the cellar'. Zelie accepted that this must now be the gift.

Zelie had developed into somebody who was angry at all the wars and killing in the world and had felt more responsibility than ever because her parents had given her the power to stop all the world's sorrows. 'As simple as lifting an axe off a hook' she thought to herself. So what was holding her back? Two things. The problem of approximations had solved itself – she was a gifted mathematician. Could it be that the problem of sorrow in the world would solve itself? That didn't stop her worrying that she could make it happen sooner rather than later. Surely it was nothing like being a mathematician.

The other thing was the precise execution of wishing and pressing. What if a different wish came into her head at the time she pressed the button? Marianna had suggested this.

'O.k. Zeezee, you are about to press the button and your wish is "peace for the world" and your finger is on the button and your finger starts to press down and just as the button goes down you think of another wish, like "I want the universe to explode" because that would be more fun to see what happens'.

'I would never think that. I only think the one thing, and that's world peace'.

'And bless you for it'.

But the thought was fatal and Zelie was torn between the two things, the thing of not acting and the thing of pressing the wrong wish on the universe in case she was the cause of ending it.

Zelie explained all this to her many suitors, deliberately presenting herself as odd like her widowed mother. Only in this way could she decide which of them should help her make a family of her own.

***

Surrounded by family at the end of her life, Zelie in bed gave confusing details of a button. She told them it was in the cellar. They said the house didn't have a cellar, it must have been an earlier house she lived in. Nor can she tell them what colour it is, what type of button or how big it is, or what it is made of.

'Bring me the button and I'll press it down, so hard, quickly. I will bring peace to the universe'.

Because it is important to their mother, grandmother and great-grandmother, all the family try to track down her previous houses and ask questions, but Zelie has moved many times and it is impossible. She asks to be left alone with one of her granddaughters and the great grandchild. 'I give you the gift of the button. It's in the cellar. When you press the button make sure the only thought going through your head is "bring peace into the world". Whatever you do, no other thoughts, just this one. Promise me'.

The granddaughter made the promise and the tiny great granddaughter looked terrified and nodded. With her last breath Zelie said 'It's never all right' and passed on the button.

The Barber

He set up in a town very like ours, a small urban centre outwith the city's heart. My girlfriend at the time insisted I should have my hair cut and that I should try the new mendicant (this is about fifteen years ago). Salifah was my usual haircutter and the reason I liked her was the calm presence and unobtrusive questioning she brought to the whole traumatic affair. Before that I had gone to a place where a girl was coarse and entertaining, with questionable views, and eventually even I had to leave because of my feeble complicity.

So I went to Skete's where the mendicant was about forty years old with a head of shocking baldness. For me it was more about the adventure now that the relationship with Annabel was petering out and I wouldn't be prepared to make the bus-ride just for a haircut when money was that tight. I'd go the once for curiosity and to appease Annabel before ending it all, she was thinner and taller than me. Anyway, it surely wasn't on the evidence of his ability to cut hair that she was recommending Skete's, there wasn't a single person she knew who had been there, and having passed it two or three times on the way to Annabel's from the bus I had never seen anybody in it, the only thing out in the open was the dazzle of his skull, and understandably this put me off even if I knew then, and know now, there can be no connection between the ability to cut hair and the ability to keep it from falling out. My sense of the order of things was that the shop on the high street wouldn't last longer than a short lease in Annabel's fashionable downmarket area.

There were a couple of waiting chairs and the cutting chair, which was in deep red leather with two large swathes of grey duck tape to cover up slashes. In front of it was a wash basin and propped behind it a mirror. No hair products cluttered the barber's space, there were no newspapers to kill time, and there were no pictures on the wall. The only effort that had gone into furnishing the barber's was the newly-laid black-and-white chequered tiles, genuine tiles, not linoleum, offset as diamonds, all neatly trimmed up to the skirting board. Skete – I presumed that was his name – was sat at the back of the shop staring into space, meditative or vacant it wasn't possible to say, and he didn't get up to welcome me, talking with his eyes only. When I asked for a haircut it was a few moments before it registered with him that this was what he now did for a living, perhaps had always done it, and it defined him from now on, so he looked at the chair and then back at me and I went and sat in the chair. Perhaps he was new to cutting. All of these aspects pleased me. To this day I haven't found a way of telling a haircutter to shut up and leave me in peace, and all the signs here were that Skete would only speak when spoken to.

Suddenly he appeared behind the chair and reached round to the scissors at the side of the basin. This is always the moment when you think the barber might kill you. There was no other apparatus apart from a cut-throat razor, and he didn't put a bib on to protect my clothes, and he was wearing a scruffy shirt and suit trousers. My thoughts veered between wondering how it was best to tell Annabel we had to finish, coming up with a better reason than I simply didn't fancy her any more – which even though it was the God's honest surely demanded something more profound – and instructing Skete what shape I wanted my head. Yet he didn't even ask how I wanted my hair cut, he just started cutting and though I'm not in the least bit vain I started to panic as to what I'd let myself in for and began to quietly blame Annabel.

'How long have you been open?'

'Sir, couple of weeks'.

'How's business?'

'Sir, you know. Relax'.

I could see the cut hair sticking to my clothes, his hairless hands in the mirror gliding over the top of my head, paying rapid attention to a single hair at a time, slipping down to the back and the sides and returning to the top, some kind of organic method where each alteration had to be balanced by the other hairs before starting over again. This would take forever. How much was it going to cost? There were no signs to say how much a haircut cost, nothing about concessions or styles. There was nothing to say that this was in fact a barbershop except the action of cutting my hair. Nothing, just nothing.

'Sir, relax please'.

I did my best. Whether it was the impending confrontation with Annabel or the weird barber or the combination of both nobody could say. After an hour of silence and my mind blithely running hither and thither without interruption he put down his scissors. It had been a pleasant outing, like sitting on a bench in the park on a warmish day, watching a squirrel scamper up a chestnut tree, very much something like that.

'Sir, I have finished'.

He didn't show me the back of my head, so I took that on trust. There was no sign of a hand mirror and from what I could see it looked more than just o.k.

'How much?'

'Sir?'

'How much?'

'As you wish'.

'How much is the haircut?'

'Sir, as you wish'.

'You mean . . .?'

There was no assent in his eyes. I had to pay him what I thought it was worth. What was I paying for? The style, if it could be called such, was what I was after if I had been allowed to articulate it, little more than a tidying up, a cutting back of what had become unseemly. And yet he had somehow divined that this was what was required. Did I pay for this mysterious divination as well? I certainly wasn't paying for any fancy decor. Or perhaps he needed the money in order to upgrade the shop, not that this would bother me, especially since I wouldn't be going back again. Straight after paying him I would be walking round the corner to Annabel's. She had bought her first house in the last month, so now would be a good time to finish with her, distracted by house stuff weighing heavy on her mind. Her father was a brute and helping her out all the time and in the house all the time and it wasn't pleasant for me at all. I had to get Annabel by herself, but there was never any way of knowing in advance if her father would or wouldn't be around.

'Could you give me an idea of what people normally pay?'

165

'Sir, it varies accordingly'.

I'd told Annabel I was having my hair cut and that I'd be around straight after, so she would be expecting me now. I couldn't stop myself from blurting out 'I'm going round Annabel's to finish it. I don't know how to finish it'.

What would Skete think of me? Even though I didn't care, couldn't care because I was never going to see him again, part of me wanted him to think well of me. He had an air of knowing what would be the best to do in all difficult situations, just as he'd known what haircut I'd required. Instead of replying he went to the back of the shop, in essence only about four feet from where I was standing brushing the hair off my clothes and adjusting to a nude nape, and reverted to his emptiness. I could leave without paying, he had said as much. Was that truly socially possible? Would it be immoral, or just rude? To buy some time I bent down to look at myself in the mirror, pretending to check over the haircut once more to assess what would be fair payment, but really to check if I was a bad person. I could see there was a convergence of valuing Skete and valuing Annabel, as separate as they may once have been. Yet if there was no connection between Skete's loss of hair and his skill in being a barber, there was even less connection to be made between what I was to pay Skete and how I was to talk to Annabel when her brute of a father was absent. Annabel had done nothing wrong, I just wanted to be with some-body who wasn't Annabel. Similarly, I wanted to get away from Skete. Perhaps I had blurted out my situation to Skete because his implacable stare and lack of worldly engagement made him appear wise. It would have been better not to have had my hair cut at all, to have left it as a skanky brown mess and let Annabel turn herself away from me and my slovenly behaviour.

I looked hard at myself in Skete's mirror and didn't recognise what I was to do. It was obvious I was only pretending to check my hair, that nobody was that vain, so I straightened up. If I left less than I thought it was really worth would I be able to look at myself again? I turned to face Skete. He didn't see me. I turned the other way, looking out the shop, and saw Annabel's father looking in, staring at me with barely suppressed violence, and I smiled with uncertainty. He came in. Still Skete didn't move. I realised there was no bell.

'Had your hair cut? Any good?'
'Yes'. What else could I say?

166

'How much?'

I looked over to Skete, expecting him to intervene. What was the matter with him? He had no interest in his own business. I turned back to the man, more than ever aware of the difference in our physical bulk, that he was what I imagined 'brick shit-house' to mean, in his forties, no time for his daughter's amours, especially this one who wouldn't get a job.

'You pay what you want'.

'How much did you pay?'

'I haven't paid yet. I was just on my way to Annabel's. Have you taken some more stuff round from the old flat?'

'How much will you pay?'

I just wanted him to get out of the shop, or let me get out. In those days less than a fiver for a cut from a barber was o.k., so I left a fiver, which was much more than I had intended to pay. It was worth it though to get away from Skete and the brute, so I went over to Skete and took a fiver out my pocket (I didn't have a wallet and carried all my money loose, what there was of it) and held it out to him. The smile was unexpected as he took it. Had I paid too much?

'Sir, thank you'.

The brute sat down and asked for a close crop. Skete stood up as I was leaving for Annabel's.

Had I paid too much? Or was it a sarcastic smile? It didn't matter, I kept telling myself, I wasn't going back. I wouldn't be coming over this way again once I'd finished with Annabel, I would be with somebody else. What's a cut worth anyway?

After a hundred yards superficiality thankfully kicked in as usual and I forgot about the haircut and mendicant. I knocked on the door, a nondescript terraced house, but far better than where I was living. I couldn't be that bad a person, otherwise I'd try to move in with her and make the most of her home ownership. Should I have given Skete more than five pounds? I couldn't afford more than that was the God's honest, not on a haircut.

With pappy out the way at the nuts barber the burden of Annabel could be dispensed with. In the house I helped with a wardrobe that needed reassembly and then told her she was taller than me, which she could see for herself was true, and that it was embarrassing for a man to be out with

167

somebody who was taller than he was. 'And it's not as if I'm going to grow any more, is it? Not at my age!' I quipped. From on high she rained down her arrogant dismissal of the worthless prick that I was (am), having seemed to store up a good fund of insults over the months, all good signs that she wasn't devastated. I apologised once more for not coming up with a better reason than height, or matching up to society's (her father's) expectations, or her own high standards, unsure if I was talking myself into sarcasm or honesty. Time was moving on and daddy would be back, so I legged it down the stairs and out the house, the memory of her body shape and exciting, volatile nature, stirring the place of my pangs as soon as I was out the door. I saw the father across the road on his return from Skete's, so moved my head skittishly to acknowledge him, and marched on to the bus stop further into town avoiding his line of sight.

The father phoned that night. I had worked my way through the films of Laurel and Hardy in the last six months and was now sinking into the delights of World Cinema, which would take another five years perhaps, depending on availability and my skill in avoiding state pressure to spend my time more gainfully. In other words, he interrupted me. One voice in my head told me to put the phone down immediately, another that Annabel's old man had the capability at distance of wrapping the cord round my neck (a time before the abolition of landlines).

'How much did you pay?'

'I gave him five pounds, God's honest. How much did *you* give him?'

'Seven pounds. Five pounds with a generous tip. You're a skinflint' and he put the phone down.

I returned to Salifah over the coming months until she was taken over by some bigger hair firm and I knew immediately without any debate that there was no choice for me but to make the trek across the city to Skete's after almost a year. In the meantime Skete had received some local press publicity, and in the picture he was smiling just as any normal person might be smiling. This was wrong. It had been tiresome to wonder exactly how much that haircut was worth from the weird one, and worse to think that Annabel's father had given more than me, though I guess he could afford it more than I could, or maybe it meant more to him, or he'd got a better haircut out of it. Perhaps he'd had a really good chinwag with old Skete himself and they were the best of buddies. Perhaps he waited for me to say a figure and he was always going to best it as a way of calling me to account for finishing with his daughter. Or perhaps it was his way of offering congratulations for doing the right thing and getting out of his life. Sheesh. Who cared? It was only a haircut, and the publicity stunt showed that Skete was no modern-day Confucius, only a barber with an eye for the main chance. It turned out that, rather like myself, he had led a feckless existence, and spent time in prison, where he'd learnt his trade. He'd fluttered around the country, setting up shop here and there, never sure how much to charge, not much different from when he started his bartering practice when incarcerated. He always caused a stir for his 'pay-what-you-will'. What was really so special about it? Sometimes restaurants let you pay what you want, and museums and galleries have transparent boxes for donations I see on the rare occasion I go in one because it's raining blue murder.

The impression that Skete was a fraud was confirmed when I looked closely at the nature of his baldness on this second visit. He was not a natural bald person. I couldn't tell for certain, having to stare hard through the filthy mirror, but was sure that there were the faintest signs of stubble making a circle around the crown, like the ghost of a monk's tonsure.

'Do you remember me?', I asked, by way of killing the silence. There was going to be another hour of this. Despite the publicity the place still had no customers.

'Sir? Many pass through. I have no memory for faces, or hair. I cut what is in front of me'.

'Have you been away?'

'Sir? Yes, "petty larceny", as they say in America. I'm not proud'.

I didn't know what petty larceny was or why he couldn't say it in English, and didn't know him well enough to ask, and didn't want to upset him by clearing up the misunderstanding about going away. Did Annabel continue to live in the area? Did her father continue to brood over her existence? There had been nobody since her and I had become lonely, stuck in the outer reaches of Baltic film. It had become obvious that I was not eligible for anything or anyone and that I had been lucky to be with Annabel and never known it. Perhaps I could go round to Annabel after the haircut, as a friend. She'd said some pretty cutting things and might want to apologise, and I would apologise as well. I tried asking myself if beneath it all the reason I'd come wasn't about the haircut, it was about making up with Annabel, making the past come good.

His cutting technique hadn't changed, a laborious system of adjustments and balancing, and the result: one damned fine haircut, worth much to those who value such things. Did he know what a quality barber he was? There was no sense of compromise, and as with the first time, he hadn't asked, and I hadn't volunteered, what 'style' was required. Once again, he had divined exactly what was necessary.

Throughout the cutting the question of payment had been rattling around. It wouldn't have killed him to give some ball-park figures on the wall. Wasn't he legally obliged to display the cost of the cut? I'd brought a fiver with me in case – it was only twelve months after the first cut rather than years, so it's not as if inflation would be part of the reckoning. What I'd really brought though were some cds I'd picked up before entering the shop. Cds were on their way out, overtaken by the digital world, and there was no way of knowing what music he liked. Apart from film, the rest of my time was spent building up a collection of 60s Brit music, Small Faces, Kinks, Yardbirds, that sort of stuff. Vinyl was now beyond my means, other than what could be gleaned from charity shops. Cds were old without being expensive collectables. So coming into the shop I'd picked up a couple of 70s Move compilations which were of no intrinsic worth or interest. Skete would see them as a nice quirky trade for the cut, and the barter was quirkiness for quality – a fair chalk-to-cheese transformation.

I got out the chair, brushing off the dead hair (Skete had no brushes), and wondered who was I kidding, to think that a couple of remastered cds which could have come out of a pound shop were adequate recompense for the haircut. I bent down to pick up the plastic bag beneath my frayed hanging coat which contained The Move cds and one other cd, a much rarer item, the first ever concept album in the world, *The Recusants* by The Recusants, predating The Zombies' *Odessey and Oracle* by a couple of months. If I truly wanted to reward the haircut I would give him *The Recusants* by The Recusants. If I truly wanted to be a better person I would give him this. I had scoured up to the limits of the bus pass area for this cd at a reasonable price and eventually found it in a hospice shop, I forget which. They obviously didn't know that it might be worth something, unlike Oxfam who always screw you for obscure materiality, and I couldn't bring myself to tell them what a treasure the cd was. Now, should I give it to Skete? I looked in the mirror as I had done the first time and once again saw in myself somebody I simply had no time for. I could look at myself and despise myself as often as I wanted, and still feel happy drinking and smoking, selling sweets in the back of pubs and at music festivals to get by, as long as there were no mirrors around. Only when I saw myself in the mirror did some kind of guilt enter into it, I'm not sure what kind. So I didn't look in mirrors. There was no reason I should give Skete *The Recusants* by The Recusants.

After the agonising and slow-motion bending I straightened and looked about. Skete was sat at the back of the shop waiting for the next customer with empty eyes. He did look wise, like a Buddha, another of his poses which didn't fool me. The hint of stubble on his skull wasn't visible in the darker recess, and I saw how his face was gaunter than previously, a sign his business wasn't thriving, which was obvious. What good would a couple of cds be to him, or even a rare cd? I would have to tell him how rare the cd was and explain he could make money from it, and that didn't appear right. For five minutes or so I was paralysed with unknowing, gazing at his empty eyes. What was in there? What kind of a person was he? The newspaper article debunked any mystification so I guess he just was an empty person like all the other empty people. If not one of the cds was any good, or even the three together, I might just as well leave the shop without giving him anything, which is what I did, more concerned now to see if Annabel would have me back with a new haircut and the same clothes she last saw me in. I blurted out to Skete 'Next time I'll bring cutlery, or cake, or both. I have nothing, I'm terrible' and left. Skete was thinner than when I entered, and it was my fault, his empty eyes, the failure of the shop.

The visit to Annabel's was a waste of time. 'You're dead to me'. This was hard to come to terms with, cut dead, as if I'd never existed in her life. She was with somebody her own height now, she said. It's what I deserved, I know. I took the bus back home to sort out the sweets in preparation for the night ahead. It was beginning to feel 'too much like work' and I was sick of it, sick of everything. Nothing had worked out and I didn't want anything to feel like work.

All of this is fourteen, fifteen years ago. I wish I could round the story off with something uplifting. That can't happen. I still avoid the mirror, and going to Skete's once a year for old time's sake has settled into an unspectacular enterprise, certain as I am that he doesn't remember me from one year to the next, and knows that I will give him nothing, although one year I did give him some sweets I couldn't shift, which he quickly hid. June came along three years ago, and she's just like me, so we get by with each other and the world in a way which suits us both fine. The final thing to tell is the kite incident, about six years ago.

I was in another part of town, again, similar to ours, heading for a prearranged sweet meeting, when I saw a man and his daughter flying a kite. This was a daft thing to do in the middle of city street, for cul-de-sac or not it was always going to get caught in the telephone wires or lost on a roof battling a chimney. The man and girl were having a right old time of it, I could see from a distance, enjoying the weather and the kite flying, singing a kite song or something, but the situation was just begging for a bad ending, tears, the lot. The man handed the string line to the girl, and I could hear that he told her to keep the kite low so it didn't get caught in anything overhead. To please her father she reeled it down below the line of the roofs and then a bit further. They started up the singing and the sun beat down in the middle of the day in the middle of the cul-de-sac. A gust took the kite close to a house and the father quickly intervened to help the girl keep it in the middle of the street. He was too late though and the kite blew in through an open sash window. This shouldn't have been a problem – the window was open and the kite could be pulled back out, and that was what the man and the girl began to do. By this time I was stood next to them, along with a couple of other people, looking up, and we couldn't understand why it was that pulling on the kite didn't bring it out the bedroom and down to earth. We spotted a man in there, and I think it was Skete, withdrawn behind the kite in the shadows, thinner and somewhat taller than Annabel had ever been. The others might not have seen him. The kite wouldn't pull free and the puzzle continued, man and daughter tugging for dear life, kite not budging. Suddenly the string snapped or was deliberately cut, and the kite was lost to the room in the house. People started shouting up now to the house, imagining that somebody must be in there because the window was open on

172

a hot day. The man went and knocked on the door. Nobody came. He came back to us and explained that the house was split into two flats and nobody answered either of the bells. I remembered then that there was no bell in the mendicant barber's shop.

Black Square on Philosophical Gas

I have wrestled with JB's legacy, but nothing has given me a bigger headache than his juvenile period. There is no hard evidence for his whereabouts until the 1920s, the time when it is first possible for us to triangulate JB's own utterances with the memoirs of others. His teen years though – his formative years – when we might be expected to learn most of what made our slippery genius – what of these annoyingly incoherent fragments? For 'slippery' is the word for Johannes the Teenager (before teenagers were invented in the1950s, about the time I became one). Perhaps we should not even call him a teenager. Let's say he was exactly sixteen years of age throughout the whole of the twentieth century's teens, as well as being sixteen in actuality in 1915, just as the century was having its first rebellious phase. And let's say – because what I am about to show you is proof of sorts – that he was in Russia in 1915, precocious youth, flirting with Moscow and St Petersburg (and perhaps even flitting to Finland to seek out a disciple of Matyushin – Blok claimed the composer became a futurist in order to look younger – how mean!, and yet, why not?), a free spirit of indeterminate heritage. And let us say, because these fragments are evidence, I am sure, that he had somehow managed to wheedle his precocious way into the Russian Avant-Garde, the very group that invented the twentieth century. What luck.

JB said as much to me on occasion when I tried to press him on his early years. Of course, the gaps – pretty much all gaps, let us be frank – have left the historical assessment of him open to attack, some seeing his later fascination with the Holocaust as an atonement for an immature anti-Semitic phase (and ditto his ham-fisted attempts to champion women's rights in the 1960s and 1970s – he surely quietly dropped this aspect of his interests when he was 'found out'). And yes, anti-semitism can be read into some of the material below, along with its opposite. I put this down to the period – wasn't he, after all, good friends with Chagall? Well, no, I suppose we only have his word for that, and in JB's words, he (JB) hated all that 'mystical crap', amongst which he might have included Marc Chagall (how many Christs do we need, for Christ's sake?). Perhaps the recurring figure described in some of the juvenilia – MaCh – is not Jewish after all but simply prone to that unfortunate strand of Russian mysticism we still see today. Yet there is a stage direction in a fragment of a fragment from his wholly derivative cubo-futurist opera *Blue Goat* that a man be seated, resting one elbow on a leg. This is how the Russian avant-garde recalls Marc seated in that mythical apartment, dreaming of flight, holding cutlery (there has been a ridiculous suggestion that this is the inspiration for Brecht's 'MaCh the Knife' – I wonder whether I should tell you this or not. Still, Chagall's 'Fiddler on the Roof' *etc.*, so who knows?). A careful reading of the opera reveals that the one possibly anti-semitic statement cannot be attributed to the author's voice. It is more likely that it is meant to represent a time-ghost utterance.

Yes, we find that JB is 16 and at the centre of the world – let us put ourselves there, otherwise what I am about to show you will make no sense whatsoever. How he managed to be there we cannot say, but he had a knack for being in the right place at the right time (except the time he was mistaken for de Gaulle in Stoke-upon-Trent in 1968). All the towering greats are there in an apartment on a Friday in Moscow in 1915: Malevich the artist, Chagall the painter, Mayakovsky – poet, playwright, actor, etc., Olip Brik and his wife and muse Lilya, Lilya's sister Elsa Triolet (beautiful, beautiful – that is, if we read one of JB's 'poems' aright, rather than the interpretation 'blue, blue' an anonymous former friend has given it – I believe it is Elsa and not Lilya who is the muse addressed by JB here), Jakobson the linguist, Kandinsky the painter (I'm not making this up, yes Kandinsky is there too), and Khlebnikov the futurist poet. Look, if I'd been making it up I'd've chucked in Marinetti (Fascist! boo!) and Luigi Russolo (the best!, the inventor of twentieth-century music – city screams – but JB had no interest in the aural world despite his love of new gadgets and pride as an early adopter of everything that could be adopted. A source of friction between the two of us).

175

What we have to do then is a search through the fragments I've discovered in the papers – not many as yet – bequeathed for signs of the mature JB, to see how Johnny B. came good. It would be helpful if we could see JB's artistic manifesto. Here it is, followed by the other stuff – I hand you over to Johannes Boanerges in early fragments.

Manifesto (JB, Mayakovsky)

'The Bourgeois Bludgeoned'

[Ed. – we only have the scraps of the manifesto – are they notes towards a fuller manifesto, or is this the manifesto in its totality?]

1. Eat raw meat.
2. Philosophy is supernature.
3. The past lives in error.
4. Only poets govern.
5. 'One must perish in symmetry'.
6. We take as we like from stoicism, and Anatolian goats.

Suprematist Poem (JB), 'Blue Goat Slap Architecture'

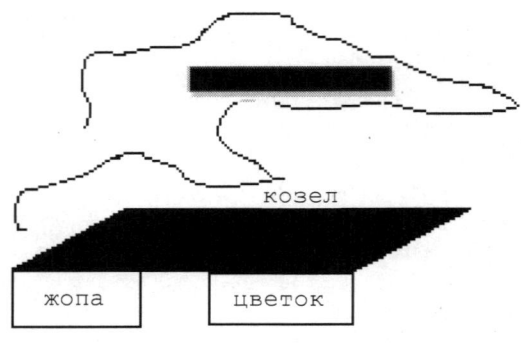

Language

Klebinov's *zaum*, the sound is more important.

[Ed. – JB's theory is that language developed historically from making sounds, and it was only by accident that humans developed language when words came to stand for things and the words became separate from the things.]

The shape and colour and weight of objects create the shape, colour and weight of the word. Words that aren't objects – 'the', 'but' etc. – are likewise developed from accidental sounds.

As futurists we must dispense with the past. Henceforth every word which has a history must be discarded. We must have only words without history, words without any past. We slap words away!

If we can slap words away, we will talk to the animals. They have no past. They have no culture. Words are sounds. Yoo.

'The dream of flight' (JB)

everybody

dreams
  of flight
      away
        from
          the flowery arsehole
            of my blue blue goat

(*accompanied by*)

the memory of perfected arsehole of goat
the perfected circular collation
blue petals dispersed into
the only future iron-clad and open

[Ed. – undoubtedly juvenilia, no mature artist
could write such drivel]

OtPla

The world of abstractions because everything
is not real. Everything is *lrea* (in Russian,
лреа), a nonce word meaning 'The world of
abstractions because everything is not real.
Everything is *lrea* (in Russian, *лреа*), a nonce
word meaning' – *ad infinitum*. [Ed. – JB started playing
with words without history but subject to an infinite regress that
happened only in the instant, or better to say, only in space, not time
– JB perhaps thought time was not divisible to a point – his grasp of
The Special Theory of Relativity, already ten years old, was not his forte.
The shorter the nonce word the longer the thing it stood for].
Words in context will be trilled. [Ed. – 'Trilling'
was a new anachronistic world and with Khlebinov they discussed a
new language made entirely of trills. There was some misunderstanding
here.]

Cubo-Futurist Opera: Blue Goat

Instructions for synesthesia
[Ed. – only the Prologue and certain fragments survive. We don't have any music].
[Ed. – a futurist chemical opera – but really more or less wholly derivative of 'Victory over the Sun' with the addition of chemicals (or chemical symbols)]
[Ed. – His personal symbol is the Anatolian goat, 'hardy, lustful. Not a gentleman'.]

'Darling' (says Pushkin) 'I have slain dragons'.

Goat: Dance on Pushkin's grave. Dance on Dost--- These are our dragons.

Goat 2: (three heads two bodies silver armour)
[Ed. – They had slapped down Dostoevsky. JB could not do the same to his idol, sixteen years and in thrall or not]
[Ed. – Instructions for chemicals to be released into the auditorium. JB lists the effects required – happiness, delirium, wordlessness, futurity – without saying which chemicals will produce these effects. This is without doubt the most original part of the opera. Health and safety existed not before the Revolution. Danger only.]

Anatolian Goat [Ed. – missing doodle].

Collage: goat with outsize Greek or Catholic phallus, covered by a blue wash (colour the lights).
[Ed. – Insertion of some JB suprematist poetry, with synaesthetic instructions alongside each

182

line — (slow curve) and (malachite) — that is, the words to be said as if expressive of the synaesthetic instruction and not the content of the line, where the content made sense. Towards the end of his life JB declared that there was no such thing as content in the pre-Revolution Russian avant-garde: 'I was a blue, stupid goat. A real arsehole'].

Direction: Goat disintegrates and departs.

Essay Entered 'The Prize for Stabilising Truth' (JB, 1915)

Frozen Reality
They wanted something like God that wasn't God. God had to be fast, high as a skyscraper, as long as it was not God. Violent like a real God. Folk colour (*says* Chagall), in Roman's apartment, not this grey – Black (*says* Malevich) – not this. How old am I? 16. I have not been born. Yet. I am the son of a blue goat.

SLAP YOUR FAME, YOUR TASTE, YOUR TOLSTOYS.

They left, shadows in Moscow, each thinking of the prize, not knowing that truth itself is the prize. Each thinking of the roubles, each not wanting to think of art as a means to an end.

WE ARE IN THE SHADOW OF 1905.
JEWS ARE THE PROBLEM, THE FIRST PROBLEM.

Chagall's face, dreamt his race. The Jew Chagall floated above us. He does not dream flight *he is flight and we do not fly*
I am in awe. He is the youngest revolutionary in a sea of revolutionaries: politics, language, the arts. All this will change. We will conquer nature and make our better selves in the world, *no longer sat in the corner inert thinking things.*

THE MACHINE IS OF ITSELF MORAL.

That would be good. Manifestoes are illogical. Everything is manifesto. Truth is frozen and illogical and always *past. the pastest. the*

184

pastest pastest.
This is my youngest future voice at the speed
of the chorus of iconoclasts. I shall fuse
politics, philosophy, art for the greater good.
The peasants have been handed meagre land
amounts. THIS has to change.
The truth is *not yet here*
We condemn all propositions, including 'We
Condemn All Propositions'.
Reality is frozen, so is truth stable? Eat
raw meat.
 'Joho Boho' (2087)
[Ed. – Signed (in English) 'Joho Boho' and
dated as if it is the year '2087']

A Ranting Syllabus (Ed. – a proposed essay? spoof encyclical?)

In order to get ahead, even at the age of sixteen (or is this closer to twenty years of age?) JB had the knack of putting his finger on the pulse and then seeking out opposites and alternatives (first opposites, then alternatives). From this period dates his interest (not continued) in the English Ranters and Peacock's gothic spoof novel of 1818, '*Nightmare Abbey*'. Imagine (he must have thought, and so it is that we must imagine) chucking all these things together in the avant-garde manner of 1915 (Russian avant-garde-ways, that is), along with Pius IX's 'Encyclical *A Syllabus of Current Errors*'. Everything 'up in the air'. Revolution round the corner in art, politics, human nature – would there be human nature at all in the future? And even at this early age, there was the extraordinary something that separated JB out from the time-ghost lackeys, his 'calling' in advance of the Revolution, in advance of the horrors unfolding and about to unfold, his wrestle with the blood-thirsty primal nature of humanity that ten millennia had done nothing to halt. Aesthetics could not deflect. Revolution in itself did not justify the avant-garde, *post facto*. He would never fall into this trap. And that leads us into what was his first ever major endeavour, an unfinished play from the period which treated the topic of blood libel sympathetically. Why did this not see the light of day? There are possibly many fine parts to it, and in its depiction of hysteria and superstition it anticipates Arthur Miller's '*The Crucible*'. We may even detect something of Tolstoy's once-forbidden play '*The Power of Darkness*', although where the enterprising JB would have seen it I don't know. It has even been suggested that he was familiar with the US Yiddish version (more anonymous personal correspondence to the Editor from a different anonymous correspondent who claims to have known JB). It has also been suggested that JB was friendly, in apprentice-fashion, with Stanislavski, which might account for his knowing Tolstoy's play (different anonymous personal correspondence – a probable relative of Stanislavski – who *must* remain anonymous) and for a possible 'spiritual realism' in the middle of avant-garde cavorting. Who cares? Here's the surviving pages of the play. As is usual in discovering 'lost' work, we have no idea which order the pages are meant to be in, so I have taken some considerable licence in reconstructing it to make sure it looks completely random. In order to have a flowing text where deemed necessary I have not indicated my additions etc. I hope to publish facsimiles at a later date for the purpose of comparison, and live in hope that more pages will surface. It has all the political and aesthetic (t) errors and (h)orrors of JB's youth.

The Play [Untitled]

[Ed. – The story, as much as there is one, is set in a large village some time in the future; the village elders are benign automatons; 5 mechanical Anatolian goats act as a Chorus, and are instructed to speak in transliterated demotic goat vernacular; the Tsar; good Christians; a suprematist poet.]

CHORUS: Good Christians.

ELDER 1: (*dressed in a shiny cubist suit*) The sun will set on our people in the villages and the Holy Land.

TSAR: I repeat my question, do you Jews make matzo from the blood of children?

CHORUS: Good Christians.

[*ritualistic drumming; klezmer; a MaChian fiddler mimes*]

***

The CHORUS separately in jerking movements brings on a child's body parts. The parts are scattered over the stage, laid out for the audience to see, the parts very visibly separate. This is an important detail.

CHORUS: (*with goat singing*) Here is Andrei Yuschinsky. A good Christian child. Mutilated. [*Elders 1, 2 and 3 appear on stage in cubist costume, move strangely*]

ELDER 1: The Tsar blackens the sun.

ELDER 2: There will be a trial of the Jews . . .

ELDER 3: . . . horses are frightened . . .

ELDER 2: . . . it is God's way . . .

(mournful klezmer; a sun is blackened by MaCh the Fiddler)
CHORUS: Christians are gcod. The Tsar is doing his best in difficult circumstances.
ELDER 3: The Tsar is a gcat. [*The CHORUS goats look in horror at each other, offended, and attack ELDER 3*]
(frantic klezmer)

***

ELDER 2 is seen burying a book.

***

[Ed. – the fragments point to a trial scene]
PROSECUTOR: These lives are lies. It is a fact of science that Jews need for Passover the blood of children to bake matzo. They need blood for wine. It is a fact of history.
JURY: He is a good Jew.
JUDGE: I acquit.
CHORUS: Good Christians acquit. Jews must lie with the earth.

***

[Ed. – this is a closing or opening tableau]
The future shiny silver-suited goat CHORUS is centre stage. The rest of the cast point angrily, pick up bricks delivered from the factory 'BEILIS' on the backdrop, and throw at the CHORUS. The CHORUS is bloodied and dies

slowly, mocked. The POET improvises words straight from his soul, klezmer perishes, MaCh mime-fiddles.

The Darwinians

I have been on the edge of music, spun by the rings of Saturn, slingshot to the edge of the Universe.

Variation under Domestication: Formation of the Bands

Frontal nozzle with terminal claw, five eyes on the head, body sections with gills on top, and tail piece in three segments (*Opabinia, Wonderful Life*, p. 126) This, the leader, Craig, self-named Opabinia, cradled in hopeless drug-addled Bromsgrove, UK. The other musical ego, seen from below, misidentified as a jellyfish, called Anom, schooled the same (*Anomalocaris, Wonderful Life*, p. 203) Drawn to dub, to punk, to house, to Oramics, to dubstep, to you. 'We are beyond' declares Opabinia, in his bedroom. Others emerge: one from under the orphanage, a runaway, Yohoia; another from under the petticoats of two mothers, Kevin, who wouldn't change, who would die young, uncherished, a musical footnote, useless. He was replaced by Asian influence – later variation, to be sure.

Variation under Nature: First Songs

Of shock: violence, sex, cussing and cussedness, misogyny. No ballads. The John Martin Apocalypse. Vestiges of what the noise was that preceded them, for they didn't invent four four or sound or conflict. But Opabinia in

Bromsgrove junked up flunky from house to house fully formed for stardom: gift of the lick and the lyric. We will set a horse running on the earth-formed. It is well guessed that life begins in the ocean, is brought forth by salty water. The constituents of the band, carbon, the elements.

Struggle for Existence: First Gigs

Only the band got themselves, and one or two fans, above pubs, an unsuccessful return to school. The social club. Bingo. Artistic integrity. Ooze. Fishes start to appear.

'There is a mystery', says the runaway, Yohoia, 'which remains. Why do things want to survive?'

'The life force? Man, you've just got to survive, it's natural'. Kevin is at home with what proves to be meningitis.

'It can't come out of the blue', says Yohoia, 'for where did the blue come from?'

The seeds of discontent. Yohoia, pushing drugs and knock-off. Opa, the leader, 'the band is all, Yo, dude. The band will survive. We're too good to fail. Nervous? Channel it, all of you'.

Natural Selection: The Record Producers

One of the all-time great producers, now something of a dinosaur, never quite *Quincy*. Said: there's a perfect synergy of talent and opportunity.

'What about the music?'

And this is the death of the record producers, that for some whiles they could overtake the music, *impress* a version of themselves as sound-types on anything.

'It was all warped, *warped!*'

What money there was bought the sound-types and nothing else, would not leave a margin for error or experimentalism in the materiality of trumpets.

Laws of Variation: Audiences

'I know you'll like it'. Yes, there were different audiences, millions of shared *qualia* and for a time it could be catered for through *qualia* collection agencies. 'Panned!' We have not more than two ears and they can follow one line only.

It is true there was an attempt to reduce to tone, melody, rhythm, pulse. More *qualia auralia*.

Then digital encoding decayed. Yohoia claimed he could shrink to the level of atomised neuronal sound consciousness and be there, intrasynapse, when musical creation entered the universe.

'You're out the band Yo'. This, from Kevin, now nicking polyrhythmia, or has been diagnosed with the same.

Op in his 'memoirs': 'K's *polyrhythmia* wasn't contagious. Unfortunately'.

We held our backs to the audience and had a singalong and a knees-up-Mother-Brown in the semi-dark, all of us. This became the basis for all audiences.

Difficulties on Theory: Transformations

Parker apologised for 'Lover Man' because it became heroin improvised. Having said sorry he asked if each brain cell was altered, or each star that each brain cell represented. Yo sank into synthetic be-bop. 'Alter-bop'. Modes based on the algorithms that generate all the stellar sonic constellations.[1]

Instinct: Politics (Mashayeki's quest for Meta-X)

There was a fight between Prince Leopold, who hired Johann for *Kappelmesiter* in Anhalt-Köthen, and the Republic of Iran, over the double cd *Persian Electronic Music* (sub rosa, obviously).

Leopold: You have stolen his subliminal microtones. I know they are

---

[1] According to the musicologist Geon, they sound the same regardless of the listener's position in the sound field of eternal space-time-space-time© (since discredited – more politics, wouldn't you know?).

withheld in the invention of a board of keys. Yet we still hear the inaudible non-scalar notes in Anhalt as the music of the spheres. We hold on to these as ornaments to undermine musical reason.

Republic of Iran: Why does Bach rule? The great court musician Barbad organised the Persian System of Modes, including 360 dastans, a vastly more restrictive, helpful way of pursuing music. And he is Bach's senior by a thousand years. There are different musical reasons.
(fight

Hybridism: Miscegenation

continues) – it is morganatic. In the left-handed marriage, who is the bride?

A machine for making infinite sounds, such as a digital electronic synthesiser, will never replace the single-stringed lute. Why is this true?

The two should not know each other carnally. Who ever heard of the bastard offspring of these two? *Heard. The Sound.* Can you imagine? A synthesiser made purely of one string, stretched over the bleached skeleton of the king's youngest child, plugged in at the child's cranial base (an alternative folk tale points to the child's internasal suture as the plug's site, pre-cracked in another tale invented to explain this one).

On the Imperfection of the Geological Record: The History of Rocks

Vivaldi.

On the Geological Succession of Organic Beings: Bands' Bones

Bach. More Bach. The Alpha, the Omega.

The resonance of urn jars in auditoria: Bach Partitas, Suites, Concertos, Masses, Variations, Madrigals, Sonatas.

On another resonance, the origin of whole tonal distance.

'But these people still host the lost world of microtonality, hear it simultaneously with the hygiene of temper'.

'Yes. Bach could transpose any piece of music on sight into thirteen sharps, the number of children born to his second wife'.

Geographical Distribution: Globalization

At last the band has made it to Japan, reunited with Yohaio. Anom is spotted in the audience. If this goes well they will tour. Stars everywhere, great lovers of the culture, no interest in the musical indigenes.

In a muso's journal Op writes his piece: 'We are bigger than all music. Our unique style levels up all music that has ever been and can ever be into what cannot be'.

A joker at the end of musical time waits for their *magnum opus* to finish, only to add another element, and so on, *ad infinitum*.

Geographical Distribution Continued: More Globalization

More touring.

Mutual Affinities of Organic Beings: Morphology: Embryology: Rudimentary Organs

Mates. At last.

Recapitulation and Conclusion: Coda

There was no music before Bach. All music after Bach is many paths away to reformation.

In layman's terms: The band has formed and reformed. The driving force that fuels the band has its rough and its peaks. What lies in the DNA is some fugue, some contrapuntal communication. The driving force – the life force – not identity, but an autonomy of music. Is only cultural evolution possible now? Was there never musical revolution?

Bibliography

Chambers, Robert. *Vestiges of the Natural History of Creation.*
Darwin, Charles. *The Origin of Species by Means of Natural Selection.*
Darwin – other works.
Gillespie, Charles Coulston. *Genesis and Geology. The Impact of Scientific Discoveries upon Religious Beliefs in the Decades before Darwin.*
Gould, Stephen Jay. *Wonderful Life. The Burgess Shale and the Nature of History.*
Lamarck. Millions dead.
Persian Electronic Music. Yesterday and Today. 1966–2006. Alireza Mashayekhi and Eta Ebtekar/Sote. Sub Rosa. SR277.

Iconoclasm of Modern Funeral Vignettes

Only one of us had been to the funeral and felt stories from his relatives burrow deep, Sinclair's stubbornness, Sinclair who knew his own mind. A boy, an early worker in the plastics factory, on holiday with his wife and children, and they brought with these photographs the knowledge that his life had been his very character. Around the bar when I lifted my head were night owls arranged in small groups, frequently pairs of people not yet in their cups. A relation wanted to be privately drunk. I kiss.

'Although I didn't know Sinclair', she celebrated, 'he lives on in your memories of him. Close your eyes and picture some moment, some special moment. Each of you remembers Sinclair in your own unique way, each of you had a unique relationship with him. This is the service he wanted and this is the music he chose'. He did not choose God or hymns.

One of his relatives is the ugliest person in the world. I tell Yarl it's not possible to separate the image of Sinclair from his connection with the ugliest person in the world. As soon as he speaks he is ugly for I remember he hates me, and I wish him dead.

At the service we listen to the oddity of Sinclair's musical indifference a pound to a penny we all plan the music for our own funerals listening to a popular song.

In the bar two couples have met, one is glamorous and young, the other is ten years older, enamoured of the distance. Just before we leave, the glamorous couple leaves, leaving us all.

A tall, well-built woman with soft features and mannish hair is with a short self-confident man. As I wait my turn at the bar I catch the end of the argument with the sandy barman – 'you give me the money first' he says and they do give him some money, collect the drinks and walk off unimpressed to sit at the table next to the enamoured couples. The altercation hasn't dampened their vitality. You have to give money, it's so obvious, there never could have been an argument.

Yarl tells me to look behind me at the ugliest shoes in the world. 'Don't worry, you can turn round, she's not looking'. The shoes are made of plastic and metal clamps and I'm caught looking.

There was an undisputed bluntness to Sinclair, he traded on it throughout his life. He would tell you what for and things had to be just so. And if they weren't any of these things there would be rifts, many rifts, a life stuffed with falling out. At his old house as a teenager there was a welcome for me I couldn't find at home, and then I moved.

We make our way to the Chapel of Rest. A louche couple, normally holidaying extensively in the Caribbean, waits in the bar. Her composure goes at the sight of Sinclair, divested of gross appetites.

The plan was for all the young ones to get their heads right out of it, meet up at one bar, and after that another, and then another, meeting up in as many bars as it took to get their heads away from Sinclair.

Here are two men, late twenties, one fattish, the other nondescript, complaining about the beer, happy that they've made a complaint and a statement of intent. After the pint is changed there is nothing to say to each other, the complaint was all there was holding them together. Sandy barman sponges complaints.

The Chapel of Rest, a vomitarium, a toilet, a come-down space. Here lies the mask of Sinclair.

In the days with no money Sinclair was self-sufficient, they all were. That was a supporting wall he destroyed. He got a man drunk who knew about bricks to help repair the damage.

When I felt within the archaic opprobrium of ugliness my bile burned.

She did not say we are cast adrift, she did not celebrate her love for Sinclair – 'I did not know Sinclair as you knew him' – his blunt character lives on. Some in the crowd thought her celebration cold, unconvincing, without authority or sincerity.

In the Chapel of Rest a lovely day was ruined. Outside, the banks of green and little crosses and flowers spelling out personal names and parental roles in white. The ushers of death that day adopted the posture of universal sympathy. Thank you. Kiss.

Yarl is bored when I say 'I can't stop thinking about the people at the funeral'. 'Down', she says, inferring the difference in our ages. Everything is more attractive than being here with me now. She wants to go to a club. 'I want to dance', she says, 'forget about the funeral and thingy and stuff' she orders me. 'You promised you'd take me'.

'Thingy? Thingy? Sinclair'. I tell her to get in the taxi and give her the money and I go back to the bar. I give sandy barman his money. She is right about Sinclair. My Yarl is stunning and the evening ends sadly with a flourishing inner ugliness.

With the images of Sinclair conjured the trick allows her to press a button without the others noticing. Dark heavy blue curtains move mechanically to form a semi-circle in front of the coffin. There are red eyes to my right, shoulders that weep. People I don't know, who puzzle me, sit on the other side of the small hall with people like aunts, uncles, cousins I recognise. When

199

we exit I see lodged on the plinth a metal contraption with large buttons for music and curtains, balanced on notes of Sinclair from the family for the celebrant. 'She can't know everybody' who dies.

I leave a message for Yarl: 'Sinclair fell out with everyone except his wife'.